Hunter's Moon

by

Jay Heavner

Canaveral Publishing

Hunter' Moon

by Jay Heavner. All rights reserved

First edition copywrite©2016 Jay Heavner

Second edition copywrite©2019 Jay Heavner

Canaveral Publishing, Cocoa, Florida

This book is a work of fiction. Names, characters, places, and incidents, except where noted, are products of the author's imagination or are used fictitiously. Any other resemblance to actual people, living or dead, places, or events is entirely coincidental. No part of this publication may be reproduced or transmitted in any other form or for any mean, electronic, or mechanical, including photocopy, recording or any information storage system, without permission from the author.

Cover design by
Fineline Printing, Titusville, Florida

All of the author's books can be obtained from Amazon.

Braddock's Gold Novels
Braddock's Gold
Hunter's Moon
Fool's Wisdom
Killing Darkness

Florida Murder Mystery Novels
Death at Windover
Murder at the Canaveral Diner
Murder at the Indian River

Dedication

To my loving wife, kids and their spouses, and grandkids.

Chapter 1

The early morning night sky was crystal clear, and the temperature was a cool, damp 45 degrees. The Hunter's Moon had been up all night shining brightly, illuminating the Appalachian hills. In the old farmhouse he had known as home since childhood, Tom Kenney tossed and turned the night away.

This was far from the first time this had happened, but tonight was different. Usually, the nightmares from Post Traumatic Stress Disorder, the ex-Army man had involved the horrible battle at Ia Drang, Viet Nam. Many brave young men on both sides died in the days of the battle. Nor were the night terrors about the tragic death of his first wife, Sarah, killed in an auto accident caused by a drunk driver. Nor was it about the suicide of his older son, Brian, who took his life on the one-year anniversary of his mother's death over five years ago. The strain of this had sent the young man suffering from schizophrenia over the edge. No, tonight it was different. A new fear ran wild through Tom's troubled mind. The incident that happened a month ago gnawed inside his head. *Why did they let him live? Why didn't they kill him? Why?*

Tom had been in and out of sleep the whole night. He rolled on his right side and looked at the bright red numbers on the small clock on the dresser, 4:15. How many times had he looked at that clock tonight? He rolled over onto his back and lay there, staring at the high ceiling of the old house. Joann, his second wife, lay sleeping next to him. She had a head cold and hadn't been feeling well. Her stopped-up nose caused her to snore most of the night.

Usually, this would have bothered Tom, but tonight the rhythmic noise had been a comfort. He needed someone there, even a snoring, sick, sleeping wife. The light from the Hunter's Moon peeked around the curtain at the window in the dark bedroom. Tom was now wide awake and knew there would be no more sleep for him tonight. He got out of bed and walked to the window. Pulling the curtain aside, he gazed at the mountain, his mountain, bathed in moonlight. It called to something inside of him, and he knew he must answer. Many times in his life he'd found comfort among the rocks and trees there. Today would be no different.

He felt the windowpane, and it was cool to his touch. He would need a jacket to fight off the chill this morn. Quickly dressing, he headed for the kitchen and grabbed two apples, two granola bars, and put water in the coffee pot. Today, even though he was in a hurry, he needed real coffee, and he needed his mountain. He waited as the coffee perked. It was then he heard the floorboard behind him creak. He turned with a start. Five feet away from him stood his young stepdaughter Miriah rubbing her sleepy eyes. She had an old rag monkey doll under her arm. "What wrong, Daddy? Bad dreams again?"

Tom went over to her—picked her up in his strong arms, and tenderly said to her, "Yes, bad dreams again, honey, bad dreams."

She hugged him back and smiled at him. "We can't have that." She bowed her little head covered in long wavy brown hair and prayed, "Dear Jesus, help my daddy. Chase the bad dreams away. Amen."

"Amen," repeated Tom. Though Tom was her stepdad, she loved him like a father, and Tom loved her, too. She had become the daughter he always wanted. He and his first wife, Sarah, had only boys. "Now," he said as he put her down, "You get back to bed and tell Mommy I went up on the mountain when you see her in the morning."

She nodded her little head, turned, and started out of the kitchen but stopped. She turned, smiled, and said, "Love you, Daddy."

Tom responded, "And I love you, too, little darlin'."

She turned again and disappeared out of the kitchen. That young lady had Tom wrapped around her little finger. He knew it and didn't care. Right now, he needed all the encouragement and love available. He took a piece of notepaper and wrote a quick line to Joann telling her of his intent to go up on his mountain. He put it on the counter, filled his mug with coffee, found a bottle of water, and headed toward the back door. Carefully, he opened the door, stepped outside and closed it making a minimum of noise. He did not want to waken his sleeping wife, nor any other member of the family. As he walked away, he heard a questioning and challenging "woof" behind him. "Tripod," he whispered. "It's me."

With that, Tripod let out a satisfied 'woof' hopped up to him on his three good legs and did a little dance around Tom's feet. "Tripod, be quiet. People are trying to sleep."

The dog looked at him knowingly and put his muzzle in Tom's waiting hands. Tom rubbed the happy dog around his furry head, much to the dog's delight. Tripod had replaced one of Tom's two dogs that died recently. Miriah had found him more dead than alive, lying in a ditch along the main road on her way home from school. He'd been hit by a car and had a mangled rear leg. They took him to the county veterinarian who had advised them to put the injured dog down, but Miriah had pleaded for his life. Tom told the dog doctor to do what he could, and to everyone's surprise except Miriah, the dog lived and recovered quickly. She just had a way with animals.

Tom started up toward the bottled water warehouse behind the farmhouse with the dog following on all fours, well, all threes as was the case. Tom looked at the happy dog. "Okay, Tripod, you can come along." He seemed to let out a knowing "woof."

Tom looked at the three-legged dog. He seemed to be content just as he was and did not seem to note his missing leg. Tom knew there was a lesson standing with him, but he was in no mood for a lesson right now. The events of that recent painful day crept back into his mind. *Why, why did they let him live? Why didn't they kill him?* They told him they would; he knew they would. *Why?*

The man and dog walked up to the old barn where Nacho, the Jerusalem donkey, called home. He was there standing next to Eeyore, the little burro taken from a passing, traveling circus by the sheriff. She'd been abused and was sick when the truck carrying her arrived at Tom's zoo as Miriah called the barn. She worked her loving magic on the little beast who slowly recovered.

The two members of the horse family walked over to the fence by the road that went up the hollow and through the gap to the big field that sat high between the knobs on this segment of Knobley Mountain.

"Quiet, you two," said Tom. "I got something for you."

Their ears perked up, and Tom pulled the two apples from his coat pocket and gave one each to the eager animals who gobbled them down. Tom rubbed their heads and necks, which calmed them. They dropped their heads and began to graze on the weeds along the old farm road. Tom turned from the animals and with Tripod following, headed up the rutted two-lane path. The Hunter's Moon was very bright, allowing Tom to navigate the road, which he knew like the back of his hand. The trees still clung to their multicolored autumn leaves. The moonlight filtered through them. Progress was slow up the steep road, and Tom was in no hurry. He needed to think, and the walk on his mountain brought some peace to Tom's troubled soul.

The first hint of daylight appeared above Middle Ridge on the eastern horizon. The lesser light, the Hunter's Moon, would soon be disappearing behind the imposing landmass known as Allegheny Front, rising to form the western horizon. Between Tom's location and the front were the North Branch of the Potomac River and river valley. Soon the sun would bath the hills with light, and the brilliant fall colors of the trees would shine. No place on earth had the variety of tree species to produce the kaleidoscope of colors found here in the Appalachian Mountains. The summer had been somewhat dry, but recent soaking rains had provided more than adequate moisture for the brilliant annual display.

Tripod, now ahead of him, stopped, sniffed the ground, and let out a snort through his nose. Tom looked at what had the dog's attention. There were tracks in the soft dirt on the road, large tracks that Tom thought must have come from a huge dog, but in the darkness, it was hard to tell. They continued up the road, and the dog stopped again and sniffed at something. Tom bent down to see what the dog had found. Scat. It was not from a large dog but a bear. Tom heard recent stories of bears returning to the local woods, but this was his first for sure confirmation. If there was any question, what a bear does in the woods, Tom had undeniable proof.

After the inspection of the bruin's droppings, Tom and his three-legged companion continued up the old mountain road. The first rays of the sun were now peeking over the eastern hills. Soon the majesty of the Creator's hand would be fully visible. Tom reached the high gap between two of the many knobs of Knobley Mountain. To anyone else, the knobs may have all looked the same, but not to Tom. This was his mountain. This was home. He stopped and looked around. To the east, Patterson Creek Ridge rose like a dinosaur back among the many hills. To the west, the sun's long rays landed on Dan's Rock, high on the top edge of the front. The colors were incredible. The maples were a bright orange or yellow. The oak's colors varied by species. They ranged from scarlet and red to dark orange. Hickories showed a hue of yellows. Here and there, the fall colors were broken by the dark greens of several kinds of pine. Tom came up here to be refreshed in this open-air cathedral, and it was working. A scripture verse came to mind, "I look to the hills from whence comes my strength." It made perfect sense when he was on his mountain.

He took a seat on the large flat rock, pulled a granola bar from his pocket, and began to eat it. He offered some to the dog, but he was not interested in the crunchy, sweet bar. Tom pulled a plastic half-liter bottle of water, Knobley Mountain Spring Water, from his hip pocket and took a long drink. His companion hydrated himself earlier from the small spring in the gap.

Tom's mind drifted off to the new incident that led to his nearly sleepless night. It started out as just another day, nothing special, just another day. He had taken the truck into Cumberland and was making deliveries in the downtown area. His last stop was at the *Cumberland Times-News* office. He had backed the truck into the delivery area, unloaded the large order, and took it into the building. A clerk counted the order for accuracy and signed off. Tom then distributed the five-gallon bottles and 1/2 liter cases throughout the four-story building. Everything was routine until he got to the long corridor that led outside in the lower level. The lights had gone off, and he was plunged into total darkness. He heard a door open, footsteps approach and then a blow that knocked him unconscious.

Sometime later, he awoke and found himself strapped soundly in a chair. Groggy, he looked around. The room was black, except for a single spotlight above him. He was in an island of light in a sea of night darkness. He noted an IV in his strapped-tight, right hand. A tube led to a fluid bag suspended from a pole, tied to the chair that confined him. Tom felt no pain. From this fact, he knew the fluid he was being given contained a sedative, a strong one, but strangely, his mind was remarkably clear.

Off to the right, he heard a door open in the darkness. Two men walked in front of him. They were dressed in dark pants, white shirts, lab coats, and their heads were covered with white cloth sacks with crude eye holes cut in them.

The shorter man spoke, "Good day, Mr. Kenney. I trust you are comfortable." The voice was eerie and computer-enhanced. It sent chills down Tom's back.

"Who are you, and what do you want?" asked Tom.

"Direct and to the point," the enhanced voice spoke. "I like that quality in a man."

"Who are you, and what do you want?' Tom asked again.

"Why, I am your Benefactor, and you will provide me with information that I want," replied the modified voice.

"What information is that?" Tom continued.

"Braddock's gold. You know where it is, and I want that information. You were there at the farm on Patterson Creek when the two men died. You were there. You know where it is."

Tom smiled, "Yeah, I was there, or so they tell me. I can't remember a thing that happened after I left my office that day. It's locked in my head if it really is there. I've been fighting Post Traumatic Stress Disorder since I was a soldier in Vietnam. It'll bury stuff in your mind, and you can't remember."

The short man stiffened, and he pointed his finger at Tom. "You will give us the information, or you will die. My assistant here has a lethal dose of morphine waiting for you if we don't get that information."

"I don't know. It's just not there," pleaded Tom.

The short man paused for a moment and spoke to Tom, "Then you will die." He nodded knowingly to the big man next to him who had said nothing. The big man stuck the syringe into the IV and injected a clear fluid slowly.

"I really don't know, I really don't know," he pleaded again.

Soon the clear fluid took effect, and Tom lost consciousness.

The next thing he remembered was awakening in the hospital with Joann sitting beside his bed. He was alive. *Why didn't they kill him? Why did they let him live?* He couldn't stop them. *Why?*

Chapter 2

Back on the mountain, Tripod, who had been lying next to him sleeping, stirred, rose, stretched out his legs with his rump in the air, and then yawned. He gave a little snort, one that Tom was used to. He never had a dog who snorted as much as Tripod.

Tom felt a giggle in his coat pocket. His phone was on vibrate mode. He looked at the number. Joann was calling, and it jiggled two more times before he could hit the green on button. "Hello," Tom answered.

"Hello yourself, you big and handsome lug. I saw your note, and Miriah told me you went up on the mountain."

Tom asked, "Are you feeling better? You looked so peaceful there sawing logs with that cold and all—I didn't want to wake you. Figured the extra sleep would do you good."

"Thank you for letting me sleep, and what do you mean I was snoring, you big lug? And oh, did I say I love you?"

"And I love you too, honey," Tom replied. "You feelin' better?"

"Yes, much better and hungry. I could eat a bear."

"Come on up here, and you may see one."

"No! Did you see one? Are they really here?"

Tom responded, "I didn't see one, there was definitely one here. You know what they say. Does a bear chip in the woods? This one did in the old road coming up here. Have you had breakfast?"

"Yeah, I had some cereal and Florida orange juice. Why?"

"Well, I thought maybe you could fix up a picnic basket, bring it up here, and we'd have lunch here on the mountain. What do you think? Are you up to it?"

Joann was quiet for a couple of seconds. "Yeah, I think so. What do you want in this picnic basket?"

"Oh, some fruit, Knobley Mountain Bottled Water, of course, veggies and sandwiches."

"Anything else you can think of or need?"

"No, that sounds good. What time shall we rendezvous?"

"How's 11:00 sound to you?"

"Good, up at your thinking spot?"

"Yup, see ya there at 11:00. Love you."

"I love you, too. See you there. Bye."

The phone clicked off—Tom was alone on the mountain with Tripod, who was back asleep. Tom looked around him. A jet was passing overhead and left a white contrail behind it. The sun was high in the eastern sky and warming up everything, including Tom. He was on his mountain, and he was comfortable here. He took off the jacket and laid it on the ground next to him. No sooner had he laid it down, then the pocket began to move. The phone was vibrating. Someone was calling. *Probably Joann wants to know if he needed mustard or mayo on his sandwich.* He pulled the jiggling phone out of the jacket, looked at the number on the screen. Strange, 000-000-0000 it read. *Not Joann, but who could it be?*

"Hello, who is this?"

"This is your Benefactor, Mister Tom Kenney. You remember me?" said the creepy, computer altered voice. A chill went up Tom's back. His Benefactor. That was the name the man with the white lab coat and the sack on his head had used. He was the one who kidnapped Tom and told him he would kill him if he did not tell him where the gold was. And then he didn't. *Why had he let him live?*

"We need to talk," said the computer-generated voice, "now." Another cold chill went up Tom's back after he heard the computer altered voice in his ear. He stood stunned. How did he get my number? And then it came to him. He'd had his cell phone with him when he was kidnapped in the basement of the newspaper office in nearby Cumberland, Maryland. Tom was dumbfounded. He continued to stand there, mute.

After what seemed an eternity, he heard the voice on the cell phone ask, "Mr. Kenney, are you there?"

"Yes. Yes, I'm here," he replied, shaking.

"That's good," the voice replied. "I was beginning to believe I lost you."

Tom asked, "Why are you calling me?"

"As I said, we need to talk."

"About what?"

"Several things, several things. You interest me, Mr. Kenney." And with enthusiasm, the voice repeated, "You interest me. The gold, Mr. Kenney, the gold, Braddock's Gold. The information on its location is in your head, and I want it, the gold that is, not your head." Tom knew it would come back to that. Somewhere, it was buried deep in his mind, but the Post Traumatic Stress Disorder that had troubled him since his days as a soldier in Vietnam had it locked away, hidden.

"I don't know where it is," said Tom.

"I believe you," replied the voice, "but it is in your head nevertheless."

"If I knew where it was, I would tell you."

The voice replied, "Yes, I believe you would, and someday you will reveal the treasure to me."

"Do you intend to hurt me again or kill me for that information?"

There was a slight pause, and then the voice spoke. "No, I believe you would have told me earlier when you thought I was going to end your life. I had to be sure. No, I will not hurt you."

"Nor any member of my family?"

"I want the gold, nothing more. I will not hurt your family. There is enough suffering in this world." Tom was relieved and surprised at the last part of the voice's statement.

"Can I trust you? Tom asked.

"I let you live, didn't I? Give me the information I need, and I will do no harm to you or your loved ones. As I said, Mr. Kenney, you interest me. One more question before we part. When you were losing consciousness, I thought I heard you whisper the words, 'free at last.' Is that what you said? What did you mean by 'free at last'?"

Tom thought back to that moment. "Free at last?" Yes, he remembered. He thought he was dying. He would miss Joann and her daughter, he had come to love her like his own, and his sons also. But no one can choose the moment when they will die. He would be free from the pains of this world, the PTSD and the pain in his heart from his first wife Sarah's death and his son's suicide. He would be free. First, he would see Jesus waiting for him, and then he would be reunited with his family forever.

"Mr. Kenney, are you there?"

"Yes, I'm here," he said calmly. "You see, I'm a follower of Jesus Christ, a Christian. While I fear dying, I have no fear of death. There's a better place waiting for me." There was a pause from the other side of the phone.

"As I said, Mr. Kenney, you interest me. I will be in touch. And do not attempt to trace this call or any others from me. It is not possible, but if you do, I will know, and I will be disappointed. It's not good to disappoint me. Goodbye, Mr. Kenney. Have a nice day."

There was a short pause, and then the voice of the Benefactor continued, "Oh, I believe you need to feed your little maimed dog. He appears hungry."

Tom heard the line disconnect with a click. Another cold chill went up his spine bigger than the first two. How did he know about the dog that was with him, "maimed" and "hungry?" Three-legged Tripod was definitely "maimed." He could have acquired this information without too much difficulty, but how did he know the dog was with him now and that he was hungry? Was he being watched at this minute?

Carefully Tom looked around. To his west, Dans Rock on the Allegheny Front in Maryland rose a thousand feet above him, but it was 12 to 15 miles away. A person would have to have a very powerful telescope to see him from there. To the south, Tom could barely see a car going up Knobley Mountain on WV Route 956. It might be possible to see him from there, but he doubted it. To the north toward Cumberland, Maryland were several forested peaks of

Knobley Mountain, but Tom could see no one. Towards the east on the horizon, about 15 miles away was Middle Ridge, but Tom wondered if anyone could see him from there. He doubted that, too. Close to him in the same direction was the mountain shaped like a dinosaur's back known as Patterson Creek Ridge. It rose gently in the middle of its ten-mile length to a point appearing slightly higher than his present position. Though it was only four miles away as the crow flies, Tom felt it unlikely someone was watching him from there.

    Lastly, he looked up, there were several contrails from jet planes that had passed, and he saw nor heard any small planes around, even though the Cumberland Municipal Airport was close, about 8 miles away. He scanned the sky thoroughly but saw only some crows. *Could this "Benefactor" be watching him from a satellite?* Tom thought. It was doubtful. He, if it was a he, would have to be a terribly powerful person. Perhaps that last line in the telephone conversation had just been meant to rattle him. *If it was, the Benefactor had succeeded.* Tom wondered to himself. It seemed unlikely he was being watched, but still, he wondered. *Just who was he dealing with?*

Chapter 3

A gentle breeze had begun to blow from the west. The leaves in their autumn colors turned and twisted in the wind. The dog at Tom's feet stirred in his sleep. A gunshot rang out close. It came from the small valley, commonly called a hollow or "holler" in the Appalachian region. The dog rose with a start, looked in the direction of the sound, and growled. Tom spoke to the dog firmly, but with little volume. "Tripod, Quiet! Be still." The dog whined once and became quiet.

Tom wondered who else was on his mountain and armed at that. *Could it be this man, the Benefactor, or one of his underlings?* With care, Tom crept behind a large rock, and his dog followed. Tom stealthily looked over the top of the rock in the direction of the shot. Through brush and brambles, a figure approached. As the person moved nearer, a flash of reflected sunlight came from the rifle barrel. Slowly, the figure came into view. It was Joann. Besides the gun, she carried a backpack.

Gently he called to her, "Jo?" She looked around. "Jo?" he called again, "Over here." She turned her head toward the call and saw him.

"Hi, handsome. Ready for some lunch?"

"I'm starving. Why do you have the .22 rifle?"

"Tom, you said there was a bear up here."

"You didn't plan on killing him with that small thing?"

She replied, "No, just scare him if necessary."

"Did you shoot at one?"

"No, I saw that groundhog that's been eating my garden. He won't bother us again. Why do you ask?"

"Oh, no reason."

"Tom, I know when you're holding back."

"Okay, okay. I'll tell you after we eat, okay?"

"Okay, let's eat."

Joann looked at Tom with some anticipation as they ate. "So, what've you been keeping me in suspense about?"

After a slight pause, Tom replied, "He called me."

"Who?"

"The person who calls himself The Benefactor. He called me on my cell phone shortly after you called."

"Oh, Tom, what did he want?"

"He said he wanted to talk."

"To talk?" she said. "He called to talk?"

"Yeah, to talk. He wants the gold, Braddock's gold. The answer's in my head. He knows it. I know it, but I just can't remember. I told him I'd tell him if and when I ever remember. And the funny thing is, he said he believed me. I asked him if he was threatening me or my family--he said "no" and even funnier was what came next. He said, "There's enough suffering in this world.""

"Tom, that's weird. Do you really think you can trust him?"

"That's the strange part. I believe he was being honest with me. Not so sure on the trust part." Joann listened intensely. Tom continued. "There's more. He said I interested him."

"You interest him? What did he mean by that?"

"I don't know, but I'm sure I'll hear from him again. Here was a pause between them. Tom looked at Joann, and their eyes met. "There's more," he said.

"More?" she asked.

"Yes, more. He reminded me of something I said as I lost consciousness when they were injecting me with the stuff they said would kill me. I was able to tell him of my faith in Jesus, how He's my Lord and Savior, and he listened." Joann was silent. She looked intensely at Tom. "There's more," he said.

"More? Still more?"

"Yes, I think he may be watching us right now."

"**What?**"

"I don't know how, maybe a satellite, maybe on a high hill or mountain around here."

"What makes you think he's watching us?"

"He said my little maimed dog looked hungry and I should feed him. How did he know about Tripod?"

"Tom, that's creepy. I've got goosebumps on my arms." She looked around in all four directions, both near and far. Joann shifted uneasily, "Anything more?"

"No, nothing more. I don't know what to do but wait. The ball's in his court. I'm sure he'll make the next move. I'm fairly certain it'll be a call, but it'll be on his timing and at his convenience, not mine."

Joann remained silent. She had taken all this in and was slowly digesting the information. With some apprehension, she asked, "So what are your plans for today?"

After a slight pause, Tom replied, "I believe I want to stay right here on my mountain and think. I need time to think."

Joann looked at Tom. "Okay," she said, "if that's what you need to do, do it. I know you. You'll ruminate on this and make it work out." She paused. "Are you concerned about being watched?"

"Only a little. If he is watching me, he'll get bored really quick. I need to stay here and think."

"Well, I think I'm going to head for the house. You do your best thinking alone, and I have Saturday chores to do." She stood, put the backpack on, carefully picked up the small rifle, put the strap over her head, and positioned it across her chest. Tom rose, drew close and kissed her on the lips.

"I love you," he said.

"And I love you, too. When you get done thinking, come on down to the house. See you then. Take care." She started through the old, overgrown field toward the primitive farm lane going down the mountain to home.

Tom's eyes followed her as she grew smaller and then disappeared. He looked down at the three-legged dog and said, "Well, it's just you and me left now Tripod. Don't you want to go with Momma?" The dog wagged his tail and gave a little doggie smile. He grunted a little "wolf" call from his throat and laid down in the grass next to Tom. "So, it'll be just you and me." Tom bent over and petted the dog on his head. "Good dog. Seems like you know what I need."

Tom sat down on an old log. There was much to think about. *How had his life gotten to this point? What had made him what he was today? Where would it go from here?* Of this, he was sure whether he realized it or not, God was there looking out for him. He had much to ponder.

Chapter 4

It was a beautiful, sunny day in the nation's capital, Washington, D. C., autumn of 1973. The Vice President of the United States looked smugly out the window at Blair House and thought how he was driving the liberal media crazy. He'd become a household word for vehemently denouncing the news broadcasters as biased and unelected elitists. Their virtual monopoly needed more regulation. The Silent Majority was demanding it, and he had big plans. When the president finished his second term, he'd be a shoo-in for his party's nomination for President. Who would have ever thought he, the son of immigrants with a long and agonizing ethnic name, could rise this far and fast? He loved to tear into the liberal media's "masochistic compulsions," he said destroyed the nation's strength. His political star would rise all the way to the top.

The red phone on his desk rang. That phone never rang unless it was very important, but who could it be? He picked up the receiver and said glibly, "This is the Vice President of the United States. Whom am I speaking to?"

"Good afternoon, Mr. Vice President," said the cold and robot-like mechanical voice. "We need to talk now."

The Vice President's mouth dropped open. "How did you get this number? You shouldn't be calling me here. What do you want?"

"First, the good news. Congratulations on your success driving the pompous press insane. It needed to be said. They are entirely too full of themselves and their own importance."

The Vice President's gruff expression melted into a self-satisfied smile.

Jay Heavner

The mechanical voice on the other end continued, "But we have a problem, and you created it. I am very disappointed in you after all I have done for you over the years. And you know, I do not take disappointment well."

"I told you. We can't be talking here. This line's monitored."

"Today, I know it is not, and we have much to discuss concerning your future."

"You can't tell me what to do. I won't have it."

"You will listen and shut up. I made you, but you became greedy, and that is not a good thing. You were just a struggling want-to-be politician going nowhere when I found you in Baltimore. Remember all the favors I provided over the years? The money? The insider advice? The endorsements in the papers when no one knew who you were? Who do you think orchestrated the split in the rival party so you could win your first election? Who do you think was the unseen hand which guided your path from mayor to county executives and later governor? Who do you think made certain you came to the attention of the national delegates at the party's conventions and then became the Vice Presidential candidate? I was very pleased with you until I found you became greedy."

"Now see here, you have no right," but he was cut off.

"I said, be quiet, Ted. You became greedy. I know skimming and kickbacks are a regular part of the political environment, but instead of getting wealthy a little at a time and running under the radar, you were not careful. You disappoint me. I know such activity is a common practice in Maryland, but there is an unusual problem. Your second-in-command kept verbatim records of your meetings. You may not have seen this as shakedowns, but as just going back to get support from those your administration benefited. The U. S. Attorney in Maryland has been investigating the contributions, and your second-in-command gave him these records with the understanding he will not be indicted as a reward for his cooperation. What do you say to all this, Ted?"

He reacted with aggressive defense and dug in his heels. "I will not resign if I am indicted!"

"Ted, as I see it, you have three choices. Number 1, you can go down fighting like Custer, but there won't be any national parks or towns named for you after you are gone. You will be lucky to get a sewage lagoon with your name on it. Number 2, I have arranged a fix. You could plead *nolo contendere*, no contest, to the charges, and pay back taxes. If you do this and it is my recommendation that you do, you will receive a suspended sentence and a $10,000 fine. Oh, and you must resign as Vice President."

"I'm not liking this at all, none of it," the Vice President.

The voice continued, "With Number 2, you will remain free and be able to have time with your children and grandchildren. Do you want them to visit you in prison, even one that looks like a country club?" He paused for effect. "Or Number 3. I know you keep a .32 caliber revolver in the desk where you sit. You could put the barrel in your mouth and end it all. What do you say? I believe number 2 would be your best option, but the choice is up to you. Just remember, none of this will ever come back to me. If any, and I mean the least little bit, points back to me, you will regret not taking the proper choice, but it is your choice, so choose wisely."

"You've always had a way with words. I don't like any of the three choices, but I guess, as they say, I'm between a rock and a hard place. I need to think about this. Can I have till tomorrow?"

"Certainly, a decision such as this should not be done hastily. You have till tomorrow, but I ask one thing."

"What's that?"

"Assuming you don't take number 3 when we hang up, I want to be the first to know. This would be a great scoop for the newspapers and TV networks I own. Again, I recommend number 2. You will be able to escape with some of your honor intact. Think about it and pick wisely. You and your family's future depend upon it."

A chill went down the Vice President's back. He might fight it out if it was just his neck, but he thought he detected a veiled threat from the other man. "Alright, I'll let you know tomorrow."

"You see, I am a reasonable man, as are you. I will contact you tomorrow, and you will give me your answer. It has been a pleasure speaking with you today. Do enjoy the rest of it."

Jay Heavner

The line went dead, and the Vice President sat alone in his plush, official office. Somehow it now felt bare and cold. He had three choices; there were no more, and he had till tomorrow. He knew the decision the other man wanted him to take, and he knew it was not wise to disappoint The Voice. It was just not healthy.

Chapter 5

Tom sat on the porch after a hard day of work. The last few days were especially tough. After one of his drivers quit at the end of a shift, Tom was back on a route until they had a replacement. He could not blame the young man too much. Jerry desired to go into the Army. When an opening in the field he wanted came up, it was now or never, and he jumped at the opportunity. Tom knew he would have done the same. Many a young person in this area used the military as their ticket out, but it left the company in a bind being a driver short, so Tom had to step in and pick up the slack. His arms and back ached. Bottled water was heavy and hard work. At times like this, he wished he was in the potato chip business instead, but he wasn't.

Overall, he had done well. Though he may not get rich, the bills were paid, and slowly but steadily, a healthy surplus was building up. His bottled water business prospered. "God," he prayed, "never let me get to the point where I keep wanting more and more just for the sake of having more and more. Help me to remember it all comes from You.

Tom had seen so many people never content with what they have. It was different if a man doesn't have enough to eat or a good roof over his head to keep the rain off, but even in the poor Appalachian Mountains, people in that condition were few. So many seemed always to be trying to keep up with the Jones. Sadly, they ended up loving the good life and forgetting the Giver of the good life.

Dear God, he prayed, *May I never fall into that trap.* Deuteronomy 8:11 came to mind, Beware that you do not forget the

Jay Heavner

Lord your God. May I never stop praising You. You loved and saved a wretch like me. I'm but a drop in an endless sea. Such amazing love. Such amazing grace. Oh Lord, may my soul sing out to You like I never have before. I've nothing to fear. You are greater still than all my trials on this earth.

A wave of peace came to Tom's heart, a peace like he had not felt in ages. He reminded himself when he took his eyes off Christ, all he could see were his problems. He made a mental note to remember this when times got tough as he knew they would. His time with the person known as the Benefactor followed him around like a black cloud. What good, if any, would come out of this, only God knows. The Benefactor wanted information, and he would not wait forever.

From the corner of his eye, he saw the screen door of the house start to open. Miriah, his nine-year-old stepdaughter, came bouncing out the door. *Kids*, Tom thought, *so full of energy*. He wished he had half the energy. She sat down on the old glider swing next to him.

"Whatcha doing, Daddy?" she asked. "You look like you were 'thinkin' again." She looked at him with those deep brown eyes set in a tanned face grinning ear to ear. Tom felt blessed having her in his life. She was the little girl he had always wanted but never had. After raising three boys with his first wife, Sarah, he felt blessed having Miriah and her mom in his life.

"Yeah, I was thinkin'. I was thinkin' about my problems and how much bigger God is, and then I got to feeling better. May we never forget that."

"Amen, Amen," the young girl chirped in. They sat there in silence, enjoying the cool evening with a gentle breeze. Traffic whizzed by on WV Route 28, the winding main road in front of the old farmhouse. A mosquito looking for a meal buzzed them. They swatted at the insect, missed, and could not locate him. Perhaps the bug had gone away. A buzzing in Tom's ear told him otherwise. He swung from his right hand and smacked his left cheek. Looking at his hand, he saw a dark splattered spot.

"Got 'em!" exclaimed Tom.

"Yeah!" cheered the young girl. "Dead bug, dead bug. What you gonna do when we squash you? Dead bug. Dead Bug." After the celebration, it became quiet again. The cars passing by broke the silence. Through the twilight, Tom saw a '57 Chevy speed by. It was bright red with lots of chrome, wide tires, and a rumble from the mufflers that brought an old memory back to Tom. Oh, how that sound stirred him. Tom drifted off into his own thoughts as they sat quietly in the ever-darkening night. The cars continued to pass by the old house and made monotonous, lulling sounds.

Tom looked at the young girl next to him and spoke, "Did you have a busy day today?"

She did not respond, so he repeated the question a little louder, but she did not respond. He looked at her closely through the darkness. Her chin had dropped down on her shoulder, and her breathing was rhythmic. She had fallen asleep.

"Miriah?" he called. No answer. "Miriah?" he called a second time. No answer again. She was out for the count. It would not be the first time he needed to carry her to her bed. He picked her up in his strong arms and turned to the door. Standing just inside the house was Joann, and she startled Tom.

"How long have you been standing there?" he asked.

"Long enough. The night's so peaceful, and I didn't want to ruin the moment."

"Well, open the door, please, and I will take this little gal up to bed."

Joann did just that and stepped aside as Tom with the young girl asleep on his shoulder went by. He climbed the stairs and turned into the bedroom to the left. Carefully, he walked in the dark room. Miriah had been known to leave her doll babies lying around on the floor, and Tom had stepped on one taken the sleeping girl to her bed previously. He found one with his toe, pushed it out of the way, placed Miriah on her bed and tiptoed out the door. The passing light from a car gave him enough light to descend the stairs as he had done thousands of times in his life. He opened the screen door and found Joann sitting in the glider swing. Carefully in the dark, he took a seat next to her.

"How you doin?" he asked.

"Much better. That cold really had me down. You never know how good it feels just to feel normal till you've been sick. It's good to be back." Having said that, she snuggled up next to Tom, put her arm around him and kissed him on the lips. She drew away after a while. "Tom, could you tell me more sometime about your early life up to the time I met you?"

"Okay, I will, tomorrow, but not now. Tom gently pulled her back and kissed her passionately. Their lips parted, and in the darkness, they looked into each other's eyes.

"Wow, it's been a while."

"Yes, it has. I hate being sick, but I'm feeling much better now." And with that, she kissed him lovingly again. She could see he was smiling. "Tom, what do you say we leave the porch? We don't want to put on a show for the motorists, and we can resume upstairs in our room."

Tom's smile got bigger. "That sounds like the best idea I've heard all day."

She smiled coyly and led the now grinning Tom into the house and up the stairs. He laughed to himself halfway up the stairs. "What are you laughing at?" she asked.

"It's funny the things that pop into your mind at times like this."

"Such as?" she asked.

"When I went to 4 H camp at Camp Minco, there was an old song about the Great Chicago Fire and Mrs. O'Leary."

"And?"

"She said, There'll be a hot time in the old town tonight."

Joann smiled. "You know Tom. I think she was right." And with that, she grabbed his shirt collar and led him into the bedroom. He did not put up a fight.

The next morning, Tom woke when the call of nature had his attention. Slowly he eased his unclothed body to the edge of the bed, carefully got up trying not to wake his sleeping wife, and tiptoed into the bathroom. When he was done, he gently walked on the old wooden floor so it wouldn't creak under his weight. He slipped into bed and pulled the covers back over him. Joann stirred next to him.

Her eyes opened, and she sleepily looked at him through her strands of hair that partially covered her face. "Good morning, sweetheart," she said and then yawned and stretched under the covers.

"And a good morning to you, too." He snuggled up next to her, and her warm flesh felt so soft next to his body. The sun had just begun to creep through the window shade on the east side of the old house.

"I love you, Tom."

"And I love you, too." He reached over and met her inviting lips. For about a minute, they laid content in each other's arms, aware of the other's warm, welcoming skin. Tom felt his wife's gentle breathing on his shoulder.

She looked up at him, "Tom, have you given it any more thought about you and me having our own child together?"

Tom stirred a little bit. Becoming a father again at his age was not something he took lightly. He should be thinking of grandchildren, not making another child. He knew how Joann wanted another child. He enjoyed all of his young children and now his step-daughter Miriah.

Joann said, "I'd really like to have one more. My biological clock is ticking, and I think it's now or never."

Tom looked into the eyes he loved so much. He knew parenthood at his age would not be easy. People would think he was the grandpa cheering at the little league game for his grandson, not the daddy. But he knew in his heart; he wanted another child. The death of Brian left a big hole in it. Somehow, God would give him the strength to be a parent again.

"Yes."

Joann stirred and separated from him slightly. "Yes, what?" she questioned.

"Yes, I want to be the father of our child."

Joann let out a little thrilled squeal and hugged him with more strength than he knew she had. "Oh, Tom, I can't tell you how happy this makes me. I always wanted another child. You can't imagine. But I knew this had to be something we agreed on together."

Joann slowly released the powerful hug on her husband, placed her head on his shoulder, and began to rub his chest. He looked at her and started to stroke her right arm. "Are you trying to tell me something?" Tom said with a grin.

"Yes, let's start right now, big boy. You up for it?" Joann said, also grinning.

"Yeah, I think so. You like to wore me out last night, but I think there's more where that came from."

"Good," she said, "but first, I got to hit the bathroom and then let the lovin' begin."

"Okay, okay, take care of that, and I'll be impatiently waiting for you."

She winked at him, got out of bed, and walked toward the bathroom. She turned and saw Tom staring at her. "You like what you see?"

Tom shook his head yes with enthusiasm. "Hurry back."

She winked her eye. "I will, big boy, I will." She turned and disappeared into the bathroom.

Tom lay there and thought to himself. *What a lover that woman could be. How could he have gotten so lucky? Was he ready to be a daddy again and at his age?* Well, he was as old as he was and not getting any younger. It was now or never for him, too. He was ready. He wanted another child.

Chapter 6

It was an early Friday morning, and Tom had the day free to do whatever he wanted. Being the owner of the bottled water company had its perks, and he was thinking of spending some quality time fishing, or at least drowning a few worms. His son, Doug, would be running the show and acting as manager of the operation as usual. Tom had breakfast and was putting together a lunch and some snacks to carry with him while fishing. The back door opened with a creak and in walked Doug with one of those 'I need something' looks on his face.

Tom picked up on it quickly and asked, "Okay, just what is it you need or want?"

Doug looked at him a little sheepish. "Well, now that you brought it up, Mister Chief Executive Officer, I need someone to make a special delivery. The order just came in, and it's a big one, a full truckload."

Tom rolled his eyes and asked, "White Tails?"

Doug nodded his head and confirmed Tom's suspicions, "White Tails."

"You sure know how to take the fun out of a day, but I guess all play, and no work makes Tom a dull boy, right?"

"Whatever you say, Pop. I just need a willing driver, and we're two short today. Terry's out sick, and Buddy's at the hospital with a wife in labor. I may have to go out too on a run."

"There goes my fishing today," he sighed. "I'll do it. Guess one of the duties of the CEO is to pick up the slack. White Tails is it?"

"Yeah, they're having a big music festival, not clothing-optional this time and they sold out all the tickets, something they hadn't expected. The weather is goin' to be sunny and hot, and they want lots of bottled water available to keep everyone cool and hydrated."

"How big an order did they make?"

"Our biggest flatbed truck will barely cover it. Glad there are no weight stations between here and Paw Paw. You'll want to take the truck through Cumberland and down Rt. 51. I wouldn't want to trust the low water bridge at Oldtown. The manager of White Tails said they have a new road for accessing the loading dock that keeps you out of the "pubic" area. Oops, I mean public area. No pun intended."

Tom gave another sigh of relief. "That's the best news I've heard in a long time. Seeing a bunch of overweight and saggy nude baby boomers is not my idea of a fun time."

Doug agreed, "No argument there. Say, why don't you take your fishing pole along and stop on the South Branch and wet a line? All I have is this one special delivery I need you for today. I think I can handle the rest."

"Honest Injun?"

"Honest Injun," Doug added, "and hope to die."

"Good, and I'm turnin' my cell phone off so you can't call me."

"Gotcha Pop. One delivery and then its Do Not Disturb. Oh, and one more thing, you need to load the truck."

Tom groaned, "I knew there was a catch."

"You can do it, Popster. I got faith in you."

"Okay, let's get on with it."

And with that, the father and son team walked out the back door of the old farmhouse and headed for the warehouse at the foot of the mountain. The dogs came up, sniffed the men, and demanded a little petting before they would go away. Upon entering the building, Doug headed for the office, and Tom went the other direction. He looked over his shoulder and growled at Doug. Doug chuckled and said, "Thanks, Dad, I knew I could depend on you."

Tom's attitude softened, and he smiled. "You always will. You always will."

It brought a smile to Doug's face, too. "Thanks again, Pop. Love ya."

This stopped Tom in his tracks for a moment. "Love you too, son."

With that, the two men went their separate ways. Tom found the order sheet lying on the seat of the truck and quickly calculated how many pallets of water were needed. He went over and climbed up into the forklift. It coughed once when he turned the key and then started. Quickly and methodically, he loaded the pallets of water onto the big truck. He watched as the truck bed dropped down more and more. Yup, this big boy gonna be loaded to capacity and maybe a little more. No way was he going to risk-taking this bruiser across that old bridge. He put the last pallet on the rear of the truck and parked the forklift out of the way. Next, he placed the sides on the truck to hold the water in. After that, Tom walked over to the window that separated the office from the rest of the warehouse. He caught Doug's eye and waved goodbye. Tom mouthed the words, "No calls. Phone off."

Doug smiled, gave him a thumbs-up, and went back to the phone call that Tom interrupted. Tom headed to the truck, grabbed his fishing pole, some bait and lunch, and pulled himself up into the heavily loaded truck. He started it up, backed out the oversized door, shifted to Drive, and preceded down the gravel driveway to WV Route 28. *Man, have I got a load. I can feel every rock.* He eased onto the highway and ten minutes later crossed the bridge over the Potomac River into Maryland and navigated the city streets of South Cumberland. Soon truck and driver squeezed through the viaduct under the busy railroad tracks. Two engines painted blue, and gold for the Chessie System pulled a long string of boxcars, some colorfully tagged with graffiti. He took a right at the light and in a few short miles, was out of town. It would take an hour or more before he crossed the river again at Paw Paw, back into West Virginia. He thought of how easy he had it today. The two-lane road was a breeze compared to what General Braddock and his army of two thousand men, wagons, cannons, supplies, horses, and camp followers had when they traveled this way in the mid-1700s. Braddock described it as "the worst trail imaginable, not fit for man or beast." How things could change in the two hundred and fifty years' time, but one thing had not changed. Men were still greedy, and the lust for gold made them do almost anything. Somewhere in the area, Braddock's lost payroll in gold coins worth 2 to 4 million dollars lay buried. And some of that missing information about where it was located was in his head. He still could not remember. It seemed to him like the information had been sucked into a black hole. Goosebumps came to his arms as he thought about this.

He passed the turn-off for Oldtown, and a half-hour later crossed bridges over the C and O Canal and the Potomac River. Now back in the Mountain State, he traveled several country roads to White Tails. He slowed at the gate and came to a stop. The man at the guardhouse spoke to Tom. "Boss said you was coming and to send you right in. I've radioed ahead. They'll be ready for you. Take the new road to the right. It's got a sign saying 'Deliveries.' You'll miss all the 'scenery,' but I ain't heard any complaints from the truck drivers about not seeing the flabby, nudies."

"Thanks," Tom replied. "That 'scenery' was never my idea of awesome splendor. Thanks for letting the staff know I'm on the way."

The guard waved Tom on, and he pulled away from the guardhouse. The new road the guard told him about was easy to find. Quickly Tom arrived at the warehouse and backed up to the loading dock. The man waiting removed the two back panels on the truck and laid a heavy aluminum sheet over the gap between the dock and the truck. He began to unload the truck with his forklift. Tom could see the operation was going smoothly, so he walked over to the office, was there for a very short time taking care of the paperwork, and exited with the check for the truck-load of water. *Never had a bad check from these people.* The forklift operator made fast work of the load. "Thanks," Tom yelled to him. "See you again soon."

The man waved goodbye, smiled, and said something as he rode off, but Tom could not make it out for the machine's noise. He drove the now-empty truck down the road to the guardhouse. The man inside motioned him on, and Tom waved goodbye as he passed. In no time it seemed, he crossed the bridge back into Maryland. It was good to be done, and in just a little while, he'd be wetting a line in the best small-mouth bass stream in West Virginia. A half-hour later, he exited Md. Route 51 and headed into the small town of Oldtown. Passing the school and post office, he saw a sign that read, 'Michael Cresap House, open today, 10 A.M. to 4 P.M.' Tom heard of this place but had never visited. Michael Cresap was a noted patriot in the French and Indian War and also the American Revolution. His father, Thomas Cresap, hosted a youthful George Washington at his blockhouse/trading post that had existed near the current old house and supplied beef to General Braddock's army on their way west for battle with the French and Indians.

I think I'll stop and see what's here. I'm on no one's schedule, but my own, and I can do what I want. I'm the CEO of this company anyway.

Tom pulled the big truck over to the side of the road into some deep weeds that needed cutting. He made sure he was totally off the road which wasn't easy considering the size of the vehicle. Hopping out, he walked up the path to the old house. At the large, weathered Maryland historical marker that told about Michael Cresap's deeds and house, stood a tall flag pole bearing three flags, two of which Tom had never seen. The highest was a British flag from the mid-1700s. He recognized the Union Jack in the corner. The next lowest was a Maryland state flag with the seal of the Lord Baltimore family and the family colors of black and yellow. The lower flag he'd seen before "Don't tread on me." The coiled snake in the yellow background was quite familiar; it being one of the classic flags from the American Revolution.

He climbed the stairs to the front door on the right side of the house and opened the door.

"Hello, welcome to the Michael Cresap House," came a voice from a middle-aged woman in a Revolutionary War-era dress who sat behind an ancient desk. "I'm Gillian Allen. My family owns the property, and I'll be your guide today. We welcome donations of any size, thank you."

"Well, hello to you, Ms. Gillian Allen. I'm Tom Kenney from Fort Ashby, and yes, I was hoping you could give me a tour of this old, historic house." He smiled, reached for his wallet, pulled out a

$20 bill, folded it, and stuffed it through the slot in the donation box. "Where do we begin?"

She smiled, "Well, in the beginning, of course. Let's start right here. You're in the newest part of the house. The Michael Cresap House is actually set up like a duplex. The family who lived here long ago needed more space, so they decided to add on. The older half of the house has exterior walls over three feet thick, so cutting a new entrance to the new part of the house we are now in was just not practical."

"Let me take you upstairs." She opened an old-style door above two exposed dark, wooden steps. Tom could see a set of winder stairs that ascended around a corner. "Come on," she said, and up the stairs, they went.

The upstairs was divided into two bedrooms that contained period beds, a few other pieces of furniture, and some clothes hung behind glass. Tom looked around. "Very nice," he said.

"Oh, you ain't seen nothin' yet. The other side, the old side is even better."

They went back down the winding stairs and then through another door into the back of the house. This part was the dining area and kitchen and was 1800's décor. Tom took it all in, nodded approvingly, and they exited out the back door. Gillian commented, "As I said, there's no internal connection between the two parts of the house, so it's necessary to go outside to get from one side to the other."

They went in the back door of the older part to a room that contained many displays of household goods and items from the 1700s. There were guns, hand tools, and other things that frontiersmen and women would have used daily. "Very nice, no reproductions here," Tom noted.

"Yes, it's all authentic. We're very fortunate to have all this in one place. While we don't have anything we can with complete certainty tie to any of the people of this era who were part of town's history like George Washington, General Braddock, or any of the Cresap family, all the things go back to that time."

"Very, very interesting. And to think I have lived here all my life, been by this place dozens of times and never knew all this was here, right at my proverbial fingertips." She looked at him kind of funny. "What, did I say something funny?" asked Tom.

"No, it's been a slow day, and I've only had two other people visit today, a man and a woman who was a reporter for the Cumberland paper. She said she wanted to do a story about this place."

"She said that, too?"

"No, the man did. He said he never knew this interesting place was here and he was very surprised, too. They seemed to be working together. Let's see; she called him….Mr. Goodfellow or something like that."

"Could the name have been Godfrey?" Tom asked.

"Why yes, yes, it was Godfrey. Do you know him?"

Tom nodded his head yes. "We met under some less than ideal circumstances. He owns the Cumberland paper. And he said the same thing?"

"Yes. He was interested in Braddock. Seems he's heard the story of the lost payroll of the General. He said it was kind of a hobby for him, sleuthing out a good story."

"Huh, I never would have thought that. That is interesting."

"Yes, these old things around, old buildings and old smells bring back memories." She smiled. "I just caught a whiff of old book smell. It reminded me of visits to my great aunt, who lived out in Pleasant Valley across from the Methodist Church near Rocky Gap State Park. Do you know where that is?"

Tom looked at her, a little surprised. "Why, yes, I do. My great grandfather's second wife lived near there. She was seventy and had never been married when they married. She had, oh, it must have been 20 or more years of yellow covered National Geographic magazines neatly stored in shelves that I used to read when I was a bored kid visiting."

Gillian smiled, "And her name was Nellie Odgers. I looked at those same books when I visited there. It looks like we're cousins by marriage, Mister Kenney," and she was grinning.

Tom grinned, too. "West Virginia and Maryland. Looks like it really is all relative."

They both chuckled at that. Their conversation became very cordial from that point. She showed him the rest of the house, from the top where tools of every kind were stored to the damp basement with the barred windows, which had once been as a jail for prisoners waiting for trial upstairs. The old house had also served as a courthouse during the 1800s. Soon the extended tour was over, and Tom bid goodbye to his newfound relative and friend. He walked down the short path to the road where his truck was parked and looked both ways before he crossed. Traffic was very light, so he had no problem. Tom swung open the door to the truck and climbed up and in. He saw Gillian on the porch looking at him. She waved, and he waved back, and they went their separate ways. She entered the old house, and he pulled the truck onto the highway, turned left, crossed through the C & O Canal National Park, and was almost immediately on the toll low water bridge. There'd been a flood recently, and it washed out part of the wooden deck. Everything had been repaired nicely, but he would have to be crazy to risk-taking that heavy, fully loaded truck over the structure.

What a strange day it had been. He had been to White Tails Nudist Resort and for the first time, not gotten his eyes full. Thank God. His interest in the area's history had again been tweaked by the visit to the historic house. And he had learned he and Mr. Godfrey had something in common, an interest in Braddock's lost gold. *I wonder if there is any significance to this? Nah, couldn't be.*

Tom looked at his watch. He'd lost track of time while at the old house. The hours talking to Gillian seemed like mere minutes. *Gotta forget about fishing today,* he thought. Supper time was coming soon, and he needed to be home. It was an hour's drive, and he had a mountain to cross before arrival. *Wonder what tomorrow would bring? More surprises?* The way his life had been going, you could count on it.

Chapter 7

Retreat from Battle of Monongahela July 1755

    The easy victory British General Edward Braddock anticipated over the French forces and their Indian allies had not happened. Over 600 of his men, Colonials and British soldiers lay dead on a battlefield in western Pennsylvania. The enemy could not believe their good fortune. Vastly outmanned, they defeated the mighty army which had threatened to push them from the strategic forks of the Ohio, where their stronghold, Fort Duquesne, had been hastily built.
    Luck and sheer bravery overcame the pompous General Braddock and his juggernaut. This time, they had succeeded in stopping the combined British and Colonial forces. Today, they would celebrate their great victory and enjoy the spoils of war.
    The Indians of various tribes, mostly Canadian and western, walked through the battlefield, looking for anything of value to them. Never had they seen such a bounty of booty to pick from. Guns and knives lay everywhere. Every Indian man had numerous bloody scalps at his side, as did some of the French regulars. The French Canadian allies took as many scalps as the Indians. Many wounded Colonials and British soldiers were killed by a swift tomahawk, or war club blows to the head. A few were not so lucky. They were stripped of all clothing, bound and their faces painted black. These men would die by slow torture at the hands of drunken, howling Indians at Fort Duquesne in the days to come. This was a time for celebration. Tomorrow the fortunes of war could turn, but now was the time to revel in the great victory over their enemy.

Jay Heavner

Chaos and confusion reigned in the retreating forces. George Washington, Braddock's volunteer aide and advisor, had managed to gather a group of the few surviving Colonial soldiers together and guard the rear of the rapidly retreating army. Why the victorious did not pursue and try to annihilate Braddock's retreating forces, Washington could only speculate, but he was happy for any shred of good fortune coming his way. All he feared had happened. Braddock's forces trained in European warfare had been cut to pieces by the enemy. They fought in the open against forces that hid behind the boulders and huge trees. The French and Indians could not have picked a better place to fight Braddock's army. They caught them in a small open valley and surrounded them. The enemy, from their concealed positions, fired down on the Colonials and British forces. It was like shooting fish in a barrel.

Lightfoot, the white man raised by the Indians, one of Braddock's few scouts, managed to survive the carnage by crawling into a large hollow tree on the edge of the battlefield. He was far from being a coward. It became very apparent in the first few minutes of the battle if he wanted to survive, he must hide. From inside the hollow tree, he looked through open rot holes as the event unfolded. Smoke filled the battlefield, and he watched in horror as men died, many from friendly fire. The enemy hid behind cover and fired into the cauldron. British soldiers responded, shooting at what targets they could see in the confusion, often Colonial soldiers who blindly returned fire with deadly consequences. The battle had raged around him for hours. Several times he fired from the tree, hoping the smoke from his gun would not draw notice to his concealed position. Washington rode by several times, trying to rally the men in this hopeless battle. Twice Lightfoot shot at men aiming their guns at the tall, red-headed man on his horse. Both, a Huron and a Canadian, dropped to the earth never to rise again.

After several hours of fighting, a lull fell on the field. Lightfoot carefully crawled from his hiding place. The enemy could return at any time, and he did not want to be mistaken for one of them. Mortally wounded and dead soldiers lay all around. It was difficult not to step on them as there were so many. Faces carried the frozen look of an agonizing death. One did not. It was John DeFayre in his battle soiled British uniform. He looked like he was sleeping. Lightfoot gave John a slight kick, and he groaned. He was alive. Quickly Lightfoot examined the young man for injuries. Aside from the goose egg swelling on his head, he seemed uninjured. Lightfoot shook the man to rouse him from his unconsciousness. "John, wake up now, or you will sleep forever."

The young man's eyes rolled around and then focused on Lightfoot. His hand went to the swelling on his head. He looked at the carnage around him. "What happened?" he asked.

"You got knocked cold in the battle. All is lost. We must run, or we shall not live to see tomorrow."

John DeFayre got up with Lightfoot's help, and the two stumbled off back down the trail to the Monongahela River. Lightfoot found a gun, powder horn, and haversack lying among the carnage. John would need these, and the dead man would not. Lightfoot was glad his soldier friend still had his red uniform, soiled as it was. It would make an easy target for the enemy, but he hoped it would keep Colonial soldiers guarding the retreating army from mistaking them for pursuers and shoot them dead. He was right. They held their fire and let them join pass. The two men joined the throng crossing the drought-stricken river. In the retreat, there was true democracy. The men of the various state militias and British units, whether Scot, Irish, or Britain, helped each other as best they could. A few men walked dazed, more dead inside than alive. Some refused to help and were cursed vehemently by the others.

Aside from a hurting head, John DeFayre felt lucky when he compared himself to the other wounded. Some would never survive this day, and many would never be the same. John drank from the river and felt better. He no longer needed help and took an active part in guarding the retreat. It was very rapid, unlike the troop's methodical journey to this place. A man on a horse appeared in the western distance. All eyes were on this potential threat, and all guns pointed towards the approaching man. It was Washington. He shouted words of encouragement to the men and stopped next to the British soldier, John DeFayre. "You, what's your name?"

"DeFayre, sir, John DeFayre," he said.

"Well, John DeFayre, "your General is wounded badly. Go to him and serve him in any way you can."

"Yes, sir." The words came rolling out of John's mouth. The two men's eyes locked. Never before had a British soldier taken an order from a Colonial. A look of surprise passed between them. Washington nodded to the man, pulled back on the reins of his horse, which turned and headed back toward the scene of the battle. The men around him moved uneasily at the awkward situation, but when John ran off as Washington had directed, they returned to their duty. They had more important things on their minds, like survival, then to ponder what had just happened.

In spite of his headache, John DeFayre rapidly made up the space between him and the wagon carrying General Braddock. Adrenaline can make a man forget his pain. The wagon had four, fierce-looking, huge men, probably Grenadiers, with guns and bayonets ready for any threats on their general. He approached cautiously and said to the suspicious men eyeing him, "Colonel Washington has requested my presence here and directed that I am to serve the stricken General in any way I can." He thought it would be best not to phrase it as the order Washington had spoken.

The men looked at John and each other. The leader spoke, "It's about damn time someone, even if a wretched Colonial, takes charge of this cursed rabble. Get on the wagon and do what you can to comfort the General. He's in a bad way."

John climbed into the wagon and laid his gun off to the side. A surgeon worked on the semiconscious General. Braddock's face was pale and gray. He did not look good. John spoke to the surgeon, "I was sent here to serve the General. How can I help? How is he?"

The surgeon looked at John and shook his head. "The General is not well. He has several bullet wounds, some through his torso that I can do little for. He continues to bleed, and I cannot stop it, only slow it down. I fear he will not live long." He paused. "Do what you can to comfort him and pray to God for his survival. I've done all I can."

Even after seeing all the bloody, maimed bodies covering the battlefield, it was still a shock to John to hear the General was dying. Often armies fall apart when their leadership is gone. He, too, was glad someone, Washington, the volunteer-Colonial aide, had taken charge. These Colonials had a great deal more skill and fighting ability than the British command had given them credit for.

For four days, General Braddock's condition continued to deteriorate. John DeFayre did as he'd been told. He kept the man as comfortable as he could in the wagon as it lumbered over the newly cut wilderness road. It often jolted when the wheels ran over protruding stones and roots the road builders had not removed. John DeFayre often felt the rocking would shatter his bones. Braddock groaned when the wagon rocked and jerked. It continued on at a crisp pace as they still feared the Indians who could show up at any time.

They neared the Youghiogheny River, and John recognized the ravine going down to where he and three other men had buried the entire payroll of General Braddock. The gold coins, Guineas, had filled the two cannons they buried. He looks all around so he could remember this place. Someday soon, he hoped to return and retrieve some, if not all, of the treasure. Of the four men in that detail, he believed only he was still alive. John DeFayre had seen his friend Caleb shot dead at the very beginning of the battle. His commander, Colonel Peter Halkett, was also dead. The last man, Robert Matthews, he remembered seeing still on the ground next to him where Lightfoot found and rescued him.

John and the surgeon watched over the dying man. On the fourth day, his eyes opened, and he looked around. He spoke to the two men. "We shall know how to fight them next time." He closed his eyes and lost consciousness.

"Call for Washington. Braddock's end is near," said the surgeon. The Colonel arrived shortly before the General expired. Washington did not like the idea, but he knew they must bury the dead man here. His body would soon become putrid in the July heat of Pennsylvania. Washington performed a short funeral. He read from a borrowed Bible. Over the objections of some of the men, he ordered the General buried in a pit dug in the road. Gunpowder was poured on the grave, and wagons ran over it to obscure its location. Washington knew if the Indians found it, they would desecrate the body. After the service, the surgeon presented Washington with Braddock's sash. Braddock had directed him to give it to Washington as a thank you for his service. He treasured this possession for the rest of his life.

With Braddock's death, John DeFayre was released to travel with the masses back to Fort Cumberland. One evening after a hard day's travel, Lightfoot found John. The two men talked privately long into the darkness. The next day they would be in Fort Cumberland. Did John still want out of the British Army? Desertion could mean death when caught. John said yes. Tomorrow, as they neared Haystack Mountain, John would look for an X blazed on a giant sycamore tree. There he would leave the road and walk up and over a low ridge. If anyone asked him what he was doing, he would tell them he had to release his bowels that were locked up, and he would need some time alone. It should satisfy any questions raised. Over the ridge, he would find the clothing of a frontier soldier who had died on the trip, which Lightfoot would leave. From that point, he would see the gap in Knobley Mountain. When John reached the Potomac River, he would tear and cut his British Army clothing, put blood on them, and cast them into the river. He must make sure one piece caught on a tree branch in the water so it could be found. Anyone pursuing him would think the Indians killed him and end their pursuit.

He would pass through the gap and follow the stream to Patterson Creek and the small settlement of Frankfort, where Lightfoot and Roger McFarland's cabin was.

Roger McFarland. *What had happened to him?* Oh, how he hoped he was not among the many dead bodies he had seen since the horrible battle. He feared and knew there would be much more bloodshed and killing before this was finally over. War seemed to never end among the nations of Europe. It only paused for a little rest and soon resumed. How he hoped this cycle would not spread here. Tomorrow he would cross his own personal Rubicon, and there would be no turning back. The man known as John DeFayre could be no more. What would his new life be like? Soon he would find out if all went well. Either way, it could cost him his life. He said a prayer of thanks to God for getting him this far. It wasn't long before he was fast asleep on the hard ground. The day's march had been hard and long, and he would need all his strength and wits for tomorrow. There would be no turning back.

Jay Heavner

Chapter 8

It was a cold winter morning in January 1756. Even though the cabin overflowed with unbathed and smelly men, this was a far better option than living in the cave as John DeFayre had been. As things usually go, not all his plans worked out as he had hoped.

Last July, John had chosen his freedom and deserted from Braddock's army. Before the British Grenadiers would allow him to go and relieve his bowels in private, they had stripped him of his gun, powder horn, and his full haversack. His cover story got him away, but there had been pursuit. Fortunately, Lightfoot had left frontier clothing, a gun, powder horn, a tomahawk, and a full haversack just over the ridge and out of view.

He ran for his life. Deserters could be shot on sight and often were. He could hear them clumsily following his trail through the Maryland woods. At the river, he shot a curious otter. He chopped it up with the tomahawk and poured the blood on his British uniform, which he threw in the river and also chopped up. When the Grenadier had found the clothing and the bloody tomahawk, they lost interest in following. John watched from behind a thick clump of bushes along the river and listened to their conversation. The general consensus was the Indians killed the deserter, and they should get back to the main group before the Indians could do the same to them. They left in a hurry and were soon gone. John waited until he was confident of his safety and retrieved the tomahawk. It would come in handy later.

He went up the steep bank to the short gap in Knobley Mountain and looked back at the Potomac Valley. He knew that someday in the future the flat and fertile river bottomland would have prosperous farms. He located the stream he remembered with the many cold and clear springs feeding it. The water was fit for a king, and he drank long and deep. The stream ran for about 6 miles and emptied into Patterson Creek near Frankfort, where his friends Lightfoot and Roger McFarland had a cabin. John was supposed to meet them, but he changed his mind. There was too great a chance someone would recognize him and turn him over to the British for a reward.

Instead of going to the little town, John chose to go to a small, hidden fissure cave in the one end of Patterson Creek Ridge and make it his temporary home. Lightfoot showed it to him on their hunting trips when John stayed in the area earlier. How Lightfoot found this concealed crack in the rocks, he did not know. A man could barely squeeze into the entrance, but it opened up into a small room that stayed a uniform temperature for the months John called it home. Sometimes he had four-legged visitors. One opossum had disappeared in a small hole and not come out. The passage appeared to open up beyond the hole, but it was too small for John's body to explore. With a little work, he could enlarge and explore it, but that would have to be sometime later.

John noticed this land seemed to be unclaimed, so he blazed boundary marks with his tomahawk, claimed a long section along the creek, then up the run known as Dennison and over the hills to another small stream where the Dan family had a corner. He knew he would run out of gunpowder in the late fall and have to go to town for supplies. Lightfoot had left a gold Guinea in the haversack. John did not find it hidden in the bottom until some time had passed. Someday he would thank Lightfoot. He regretted not going to him. He waited while his thick beard and hair grew out to change his looks, and the ruse worked. No one in town recognized him, and Lightfoot, he was told, was out long hunting with Roger. He was glad Roger survived, though they also said he was recovering from a wound.

The Governor of Virginia commissioned a string of forts to be constructed along the entire western frontier of the state for protection from the French and Indian hordes. Colonel George

Washington was given the monumental task of seeing this was done, but the state government provided little money.

Men were needed as workers and soldiers. John signed on with great enthusiasm under his new identity as John Phares and was now part of the group Colonel Bacon directed. Many men and women changed their names to escape their past during these tumultuous times. The commander was having better luck with the fort building than turning the motley group into soldiers. John's experience in the British Army helped him understand the soldier training, but he was careful not to reveal he knew too much. Suspicions could be aroused, and he did not want questions asked about his past.

The men were busy building the fort's palisades and a second cabin for housing and storage when Colonel Washington rode in, and he was not happy with what he saw. His face spoke volumes. He walked into the cabin that Lieutenant Bacon used as an office when the men were not sleeping in it. Washington had a temper that went with his red hair, and from the loud yelling, the men could tell Bacon was being raked over the coals. It was hard to understand precisely what was said, but the men knew they would be the next to feel the pain once Colonel Washington was done chewing on Bacon. The yelling stopped, and the two men could be heard talking, but no one outside was sure what they were saying. The discordant sounds from the two continued for about ten more minutes, then abruptly stopped.

Bacon came swiftly out of the cabin with the Colonel following closely. The Lieutenant ordered the men to fall-in, which they did in a crooked line with haste. Washington was not pleased and began yelling at the men. It was made straight as they jumped at his commands. The Colonel walked down the line slowly. He stopped at each man, asked his name, and looked him over like one vets a horse. John heard several men cough nervously and twist slightly as the Colonel's steely gaze met their eyes. Several looked like they would wet their breeches. Washington worked his way down the line and stopped in front of John Phares. He said nothing as he looked him over from head to toe. His eye contact seemed to go right through John. *Did Washington remember him as John DeFayre,*

British soldier and deserter? He stared for what seemed like forever to John, then turned and worked his way down the line. John gave a slight sigh of relief. Perhaps his secret was safe.

When he finished his inspection, he walked to Bacon, turned, and began to address the troops. "Men," he said. "I am sure you noticed I was not pleased with what I saw when I arrived here. There were no guards posted. Your weapons are still all in the cabin. A hand-full of French and their bloody Indian allies could kill all you all and leave with your scalps on their belts. Never again will this oversight happen. There is to be constant patrolling of this fort by a minimum of two men at day and night every day until this war is over. Drunkenness and slothfulness will not be tolerated. I've authorized Lieutenant Bacon the use of the lash for such offenses, and also, deserters will be hung or shot."

A gasp went through the men. John felt the Colonel had been looking straight at him when he said the last phrase. He felt like running, but his legs seemed frozen in place.

Washington went on. "As you know, this is one of a string of forts the Governor of Virginia has ordered built down the mountains and valleys paralleling the Shenandoah and South Branch of the Potomac and beyond the New River far south of here. Some of you will be called upon if needed to build these additional forts. All of you are expected to be prepared for battle. Lieutenant Bacon has assured me you will be ready for this yesterday." He looked at Bacon, who swallowed hard. "I have nothing more to say," said the Colonel. "Return to your work except for the two men at the end of the line on my right who will be on guard duty. Lieutenant Bacon will assign guard duty after this. You are dismissed."

The men began to disperse and walk off when Washington's booming voice rang out. "Mr. Phares, I need to speak with you privately."

John felt his heart leap in his chest. He feared the worst as he walked to the Colonel's position. He could feel Washington's steely eyes on him, but John could not make eye contact. He stood in front of the tall red-headed man in the tricorn hat and looked at his feet. "Mr. Phares, come with me."

John followed the Colonel closely behind. He felt like a condemned man heading to the gallows. Perhaps he was. Washington walked through the palisades where a gate was being built. They walked at least 150 feet to a thick clump of trees and went around to the backside. Maybe he will shoot me as an example to the others. Washington turned to him, but no pistol was in his hand, though John saw one at the Colonel's side.

"Mr. DeFayre, I last saw you in a red British uniform on Braddock's ill-fated endeavor. I see you have taken a new name and identity, but I could never forget those eyes after our encounter after the battle near the Monongahela River. You seem to be adjusting well." John said nothing. He had been caught and resigned himself to his fate. "Don't look so glum, Mr. Phares. I've heard nothing but good reports about you."

John looked at the Colonel, "Aren't you going to have me hung or shoot me yourself?"

Washington smiled, "No. If I hung every man in my army who'd recently left the British Army under, shall we say 'not the best of circumstances;' we would have time for nothing but building gallows. Lieutenant Bacon speaks highly of you, and I need men with military experience. Your secret is safe with me as long as you do not desert, and if you do, you will hang." The Colonel let the last statement sink in. He continued, "I have a special assignment, and I would like you to help me with that. Would you be interested in that, Mr. Phares?"

"Yes, very much, Colonel Washington. Very much. You can count on me."

"I thought that would be your answer when I first spotted you here. I've placed my trust in you. Don't let me down."

John told the Colonel he had not made a mistake with his trust. He was to travel to Fort Cumberland with the Colonel, and there he would be given his assignment. The two men talked as they went back to the fort about how it was progressing. John received some questioning looks from the other men when he went back to work.

The rest of the day went quickly as the men worked with renewed vigor. Night fell early in the winter. The cook made some watery soup for the hungry men's supper along with cornbread, which they ate quickly. Soon all were asleep except for two guards. And guns were ready and loaded if needed this night. Bacon made sure this was done.

In the morning, Washington rode out on his horse, followed by John Phares, also on a horse, though he was not near as graceful as the Colonel. The only other time he had ridden in his life was when the gold coin payroll was buried near the Youghiogheny River in Pennsylvania. He would have to learn fast. Washington had an assignment for him, and John was curious what it was about. Speculating did little good. The Colonel was tight-lipped. He would have to wait until Washington was ready.

Jay Heavner

Chapter 9

For the next two years, John Phares served as George Washington's aide and confident. Young Washington was an ambitious man who desired to make a name for himself. What man at that age didn't? There was an ongoing conflict at Fort Cumberland between Washington and Captain John Dagsworth. Dagsworth was from Maryland and held the title of Captain in the British Army; thus, he believed he outranked the colonial militia colonel. Washington had more political connections and came out on top. John remained loyal to Washington but stayed out of the quarrel. Dagsworth, to his credit, took his defeat honorably and continued to serve admirably, though Washington seemed to continue to hold ill feelings toward the man.

John Phares carried letters and instructions from Colonel Washington to the frontier forts all along the ridges and valleys the length of Virginia and once traveled to North Carolina with a message he delivered to the commander at Fort Dobbs who eagerly received it. He also went to nearby Maryland and Pennsylvania forts. Numerous times he ran from the French and Indians who continued to wreak havoc on the thinly guarded frontier. The undermanned and undersupplied forts and blockhouses were the only things keeping the enemy from completely overrunning the Colonial areas. Few settlers had managed to hold out. Most fled to Winchester, Frederick, or Philadelphia or been killed. Many times he passed ruined farms and manors in the fertile valleys. One, in particular, stood out in his mind. A cabin in the Patterson Creek Valley belonged to a family he knew, and it was still on fire when he arrived. The father, mother, and 3 of their children were all dead and scalped. The two smallest children were missing, probably carried off by the Indians. He could tell there had been a terrible fight. Two dead Indians lay in the woods nearby. John wanted to bury the dead but did not. The Indians were still near. Why they had not carried off their dead as usual, he did not know. Never had he been able to get the images of his dead neighbor from his mind, even a year later. His decision to not bury them would trouble him for the rest of his life.

Just recently, he had returned from the South Fork area near the fertile headwaters of a branch of the Potomac River. Fort Seybert had been overrun by the Delaware Indian Chief Killbuck and his braves. Many died on that April day or been captured and carried off. This was far from the first time John had seen Killbuck's handiworks. He hoped it would be the last.

Today he carried a letter from Colonel Bouquet, busy in Raytown, Pennsylvania, building a depot and fort called Fort Bedford to house British General John Forbes's growing army. Colonel Washington sent John with a letter to Bouquet outlining his plans for an invasion of the French-occupied lands to the west and the conquest of their stronghold, Fort Duquesne, at the strategic forks of the Ohio River. Washington was anxious for a reply.

The answer had not pleased Colonel Washington at all. He was furious. Why would General Forbes want to consider cutting an entirely new road through the Pennsylvania wilderness when they already had the upgraded road Braddock so painstakingly cut from Cumberland, Maryland, almost to the forks of the Ohio? It was sheer madness. Hadn't he learned how difficult it was constructing a new road through the wilderness from Shippensburg to Raytown on the Juniata River? It would be far better time-wise and involve much less effort to use the existing road. John also knew the Virginian Washington did not want to have another route in a neighboring state to compete for trade in the Ohio valley and the way further west into the continent.

Furthermore, Washington was ordered to improve the road from Cumberland north up the valley to Raytown. This he would do without question. The roadway could be used by Forbes's forces to come south and then take the route Braddock built almost to the forks. The Colonel was still interested in a commission in the British Army, and he would follow his orders whether he liked them or not.

Washington's forces from Virginia and Maryland set to work widening the old Indian trail to Raytown. Both the Colonel and John Phares were surprised at how rapidly the combined forces completed the task. Washington met with General Forbes and Colonel Bouquet and pleaded his case for using the existing road while Bouquet favored a new and shorter road to the French stronghold. Bouquet's scouts had informed him that while challenging, it was possible to secure a passage through the remaining hills and valley to their objective. The final decision was General Forbes, and he sided with Bouquet much to Washington's displeasure. Construction began on the new route. Forbes also had some of Washington's men continue to improve Braddock's Road from Cumberland. This would cause the French to divide their already thin lines. They would have no way of knowing from which avenue the sizeable British force would attack.

There were other problems the British forces faced besides hills, ravines, streams, and deep marches that threatened to swallow men, horses, and wagons. Forbes was plagued by intestinal issues before, and they had returned to him. He was also worried about the possibility of attacks along the journey west by local Delaware and Shawnee. Pennsylvania authorities appointed Frederick Post, a Moravian missionary who spoke Delaware, to persuade the local tribes the army, growing more significant daily, was only interested in driving out the French and would not impose on them or their homeland.

At considerable personal risk, Post was able to convince the chiefs of this. He went east over the mountains and returned with a peace belt and a copy of the treaty assuring the Indians of British sincerity. Forbes had learned from Braddock's mistake of insulting and dismissing the native tribes. Braddock had only nine native scouts who did not leave. Forbes also wisely took Washington's advice and accepted the services of 600 Cherokee and Catawba Indians, mortal enemies of the northern Indians. Washington wondered to himself if Forbes, being a Scot instead of a bullheaded Englishman like Braddock, made him more open to suggestions from others. General Braddock's arrogance had led to his own death and hundreds of others.

While Post was working his magic, Bouquet pressed westward over Laurel Ridge to Loyalhanna Creek. He arrived on September 7 and met Colonel James Burd, commanding one of the Pennsylvania battalions. Together, they erected another outpost and named it Fort Ligonier after General John Ligonier, a relative of Prime Minister William Pitt, who had authorized the campaign against the French. Forbes also realized he needed defensible places to fall back to quickly if his forces ran into trouble. Braddock had no such contingencies. This had been one big factor in his rout. They were within a scant fifty miles of Fort Duquesne and felt confident of success, much like Braddock had several years earlier.

A few short days later, Bouquet sent a reconnaissance force of 850 under the command of a headstrong man by the name of Major James Grant out toward the forks. Grant's bungling, when he met a French and Indian force, resulted in his capture and the loss of 300 men. Bouquet was distraught by the setback, but the British forces still totaled over 6,000. He could afford to lose a few. Despite the defeat, the spirits of the troops remained high. They were very near the source of despair for the frontier settlers. It has been a long, torturous summer for the ones who stayed.

The French and Indians continued to harass and sometimes attack Fort Ligonier throughout September and October. Each time they failed and returned to Fort Duquesne, realizing the only thing that would stop the British juggernaut was the rapidly approaching winter, but the British did not know that.

It was not until November 2 that General Forbes, pale and emaciated from the disease wracking his intestines, reached Fort Ligonier. The weather took a turn for the worse, and he and the war council must make a hard choice. Should they press on to the forks of the Ohio or fall back and try again in the spring? The men, including George Washington and John Phares, reluctantly decided to wait.

Jay Heavner

The next evening, scouts came running into the fort and reported a French raiding party was sighted close to the fort. Lt. Col. George Mercer led a detachment of Virginians out to find and engage the enemy. They did, and a sharp skirmish ensued. Colonel George Washington was ordered by General Forbes to take another detachment of Virginia troops and support Mercer. Darkness continued to fall, and a fog arose, making visibility even worse. Washington's forces cautiously approached the scene, but Mercer's men mistook them for the French and opened fire. Washington's men returned fire. Colonel Washington quickly realized the mistake and ran between the two forces ordering the men to cease fire. Before the fighting stopped, 14 Virginians died from friendly fire. The Colonel later confessed to John Phares that never in his life had he been so scared. John Phares, who was with him that deadly night, quickly agreed.

But all was not lost for the Virginians that night. They managed to capture 3 of the French. One was an English deserter who described the French position at their fort as desperate. Provisions and morale were low. Many soldiers left for winter quarters at other French fortifications, and there was more bad news for the French, but good for Forbes. The French's Indian allies had nearly all left. Some chose to winter at their villages, and others, who had seen the massive English force, deserted the seemingly hopeless situation. With this bit of information, General Forbes pressed a final push to seize the vital forks of the Ohio.

On November 24, his army was only a day's march from their objective. Indian scouts returned with news of smoke billowing from the directions of the French fort. Forbes sent cavalry ahead of the main force to report on conditions at the vital point. They found the French had destroyed everything they could not carry and burned the fort. Forbes arrived the next day and sent word to William Pitt of his success in capturing the forks. The British forces built a large fort there and kept it well manned. General Forbes had little time to enjoy this good fortune and would die from his ailment soon afterward.

Washington returned to Raytown with the Army and then retired to his home in Virginia. John Phares received permission to return to Fort Cumberland via Braddock's Road. He took two horses with him, and in a small ravine near the Youghiogheny River, and he returned to a spot only he knew about. He dug till he found two buried cannons and stuffed his saddlebags full of gold, Braddock's gold. When he could carry no more, he filled in the hole and carefully covered it. John Phares looked around making careful note of landmarks. There was much more gold to retrieve later.

John traveled through the woods of Pennsylvania and Maryland without incidence. Near Haystack Mountain, he took the path he used when he deserted from Braddock's Army. How things had changed from that day. His horse stumbled, going up the steep bank from the Potomac and nearly fell with him on it. Fortunately, it recovered its footing. A fall here would have killed them both. He went through the short gap with the gushing springs from which both he and the horse drank till they were full. The stream led them to Patterson Creek. They forded the cold, icy stream carefully, and John was soon at his plot he had claimed by tomahawk rights. He went to the hidden fissure cave he once called home and buried the gold under rocks. If he had been alone, he would have slept in the cave, but he had two horses to worry about. Wolves and mountain lions might desire to make a meal of his animals, and he did not want to see that happen, so he slept in a crude lean-to shelter. Tomorrow he'd go to Fort Cumberland and receive his official discharge from the army. He'd use a little of his newfound wealth to purchase supplies and tools for building the barn and then his cabin. He and his animals would live in the barn until he could get his cabin finished. And all the time, he'd be thinking about what to do with the gold, Braddock's gold.

Jay Heavner

Chapter 10

Two years passed since John Phares left his position as Colonel Washington's aide. They were very productive years. With help from neighbors, he erected a small barn and cabin. Gone was the lean-to first used for shelter. He no longer needed the cave, though, on hot summer nights, he sometimes wondered if sleeping in the cool, damp hole may not be a good idea. The harvest from the land he cleared was good. Ample rains had fallen when needed, and his animals increased their number. Somewhere in the hills around him, his pigs were fattening themselves on chestnuts, acorns, and any small creatures not faster than the pig's hungry mouths.

His pregnant wife Jenny would deliver soon, and he wanted to make the trip to the Youghiogheny River in Pennsylvania as short as possible. She was not happy with him leaving as her time drew near, but it was the best time in the year to get ginseng which had grown big and fat during the summer. The weather would take a turn for the worst in the near future, and travel would be difficult if not impossible. Going for ginseng root meant some quick cash and provided a reason for his journey to where it grew abundantly on the high plateau. A neighbor woman, the widow Wagoner, would stay with Jenny in his absence and help out. He needed to get the gold, Braddock's gold, buried near the river while the frontier was peaceful. How long it would last, he did not know. Even though the French were defeated, the many tribes of Indians still were a formidable force and a threat to the settlers in the eastern Appalachians.

John traveled swiftly over the improved trails Braddock's forces cut for his Army before the rout at the forks of the Ohio. Colonel Washington's men upgraded it further in 1758 on orders from General Forbes. Forbes had not used this route on his march to the forks, but instead cut a new route through the highlands of Pennsylvania much to Washington's dismay and protest. Just the same, it made John's journey easier on the way west to the buried treasure.

He pushed himself and his two horses hard and made the trip in two days. On the morning of the third day, John found the secluded spot near the Youghiogheny River and dug up all the gold coins he could carry on the two animals. He filled in the hole which exposed the ends of cannons holding Braddock's missing payroll and covered it carefully leaving little evidence the ground had been disturbed. The falling leaves of autumn would complete the hiding.

After noon, he returned along the same river toward home. He was not sure what he would tell Jenny about coming home empty-handed without some ginseng. The pregnant woman was not moving far from the house, and he knew he could get the gold to the fissure cave without her knowing, but what would he tell her about having no ginseng? There was plenty in the woods, but the harvesting of the plants by the local settlers had made it scarcer. Somehow, he did not think she'd believe him if he told her he found none. He knew of men, some of the long hunters, who had other women besides their wives when they lived away from home and also had children with them. He hoped she trusted him better than that, but still, she might wonder.

Somewhere ahead of him, he heard a crying that raised the hair on the back of his neck. A horse was screaming in pain, and the noise seemed to be coming from the river. He hurried forward and found a man trying to right a downed horse with a heavy load at a fording place. John tied his horses and ran into the stream to help the man and horse. There was no time for introductions, and the man was more than happy with unexpected help. Together they got the heavily burdened horse up and out of the swift-flowing water. They were exhausted when they reached the dry river bank and sat down breathing heavily. The other man was dressed like a typical frontiersman. Somehow, he had managed to keep his felt hat on during the confusion. He wore a buckskin frock, breeches, and moccasins. Between his pants, he spoke to John. "Thank you," he said. "Thank you. I thought I had lost my horse and ginseng." He stopped to catch his breath. "Name's Dan'l Boone. Sorry, I don't know yours, but I know a friend when I see one."

"You're welcome." John took another much-needed breath. "You looked like you could use some help, and it was me or nothin'." He took another breath. "Name's John, John Phares. It's good to meet you, Dan'l, or is it Daniel Boone?"

"It don't make much diff'rance what you call me, just as long as you don't forgit to call me for supper." They chuckled at the joke.

Daniel went on, "I'm much obliged for your help. Say you look familiar. Were you with General Braddock on his march here five years ago? It sure seems to me our paths have crossed somewheres before."

John could feel his stomach churn. He was still worried someone would recognize him from his time in the British Army. To them, he was a deserter with a price on his head. John spoke carefully. "You know, you're not the first person who's told me that. Somewheres out here, I have a twin from another mother."

Boone laughed at that. "Yeah, they tell me that me and my cousin Daniel Morgan look a lot alike, and havin' the same first name don't help."

John said, "I think I may have met Morgan. Perhaps you recognize me from General Forbes campaign to the forks of the Ohio 2 years ago, or maybe I met you when I was Colonel Washington's aide. I carried messages to the frontier forts all over Virginia and even made it to Fort Dobbs in North Carolina."

Boone looked at him carefully. "Guess it could have been any of those. I got kinfolk down on the Yadkin River in North Carolina. Just the same, you done me a big favor today, and for that, I call you 'friend.' I owe you one. You appear to me as a man I can trust. Ain't too many woulda done what you done for me just now."

"Thank you," John said. "Friends are always good to have here on the frontier. Which way are you going with that load of ginseng?"

"I'm heading for Winchester, Virginia. I heard tell they're payin' top price for it there. And you, which way are you headin'?"

"I'm headin' the same direction, but I'm only goin' as far as Ashby's Fort cross the Potomac nears to Fort Cumberland. What you say we travel together? There's still some unsavory characters roaming these woods, and there's safety in numbers."

"You make a good point. I'd be happy to have you as a trav'lin' partner."

And so it was. Over the next three days, the two men made their way to John's home. John showed Daniel Boone the short cut he knew to Winchester via the gap in Knobley Mountain. On the second day, he also thought of an idea that would help him and Boone.

"Dan'l, he said. "I could use your help. I have my own reasons for traveling to Pennsylvania, and I told my wife I was goin' for ginseng. You have some, and I need it. Would you consider 'rentin' it to me?"

Boone looked at him curiously. "I know we all have reasons for doin' what we do, and I can understand a man wantin' to keep them to hisself, but I don't reckon I know why or what you mean by 'rentin' my ginseng. I think I'd like to hear a little more explanation of this."

"What I can tell you is this. I told my wife I was going for ginseng. If I come back without it, she's gonna wonder why. You have ginseng, and I don't. Can I 'rent' it from you for a short while? I can pay you in gold for what the ginseng is worth and then some more as 'rent.' When we get to my cabin, you'll buy it from me with the gold I gave you, but you keep the 'rent' money and ask no questions. You can then take the ginseng to Winchester and sell it."

Boone rubbed his chin as he pondered this idea. He smiled, "You know, if it hadn't been for you, I wouldn't have that ginseng and probably not the horse either. I guess a man has a reason for everything and some he can keep to hisself, so Mr. Phares if you want to 'rent' my ginseng, I'm gonna let you under those generous terms you just proposed. I'm a man of my word, and I believe you are, too. Let's shake on it," and they did.

Jay Heavner

When they got to John's cabin on the side of the hill, Jenny greeted them. She said she was having mild contractions, and the neighbor had gone for the midwife. John kissed her and walked her to the porch. He and Boone quickly exchanged the ginseng and gold as they had agreed. Out of Jenny's hearing, he told Boone he'd like to do this yearly if possible. Boone thought about it, agreed, and the two men shook on it. He left for Winchester shortly afterward with directions containing another short cut that John knew.

Later that night, with help from the midwife, Jenny gave birth to a girl they named Jasmine. John wasn't much of a praying man, though he knew the Good Lord watches over everyone from above. All in the cabin bowed their heads as he prayed, "Dear Lord, thank you for this new life, this child you have given us. Keep her healthy and safe from this day forward. Watch over my friend Boone. He needs it as we all do now and forever. Again, thank you for this child and my safe return home. Please keep Your eye on us. I know You watch over the tiny sparrow, and You'll watch out for us. Amen."

All present said 'amen' in agreement. Little could John know how his prayer would be answered.

Chapter 11

On an early spring morning in 1772, with the sun was just peeping over Middle Ridge to the east, John Phares sat on the porch of his old one-room log cabin just like he had the day before, but things would never be the same. Injun Joe was dead, and John had nearly lost his whole family yesterday on the worst day of his life.

The day started out like any other day. He awoke to find his wife's warm body snuggled up next to him. It had been 12 years since he'd bought her indentured servant papers from Mr. Durham, a pompous Englishman passing through. John paid Durham far more than he needed to, but he wanted the man to go far away and never to come back. He had not returned, and John believed Durham dead.

John had found Jenny beautiful the first time he saw her, even though she wore a soiled dress and had uncombed hair. As a Christmas present, he'd torn her bondage papers up and given her freedom. She chose to stay and became his wife. He felt blessed as she had. Five little Phares children now ran around the homestead with Jasmine, aged 11, being the oldest.

This morn, Jenny woke early, also and the two consummated their love in the dark cabin before the children awoke. After Jenny went back to sleep, John put on his clothes and slipped out the door to the porch. He sat in a dark silence broken by a distant whippoorwill's repeated call. He heard the door open, and five-year-old Billy walked out. His nightshirt nearly touched the ground. He yawned, stretched, and plopped down on the hard bench next to his father.

"Hi, little man. You're up early," said John. "Couldn't you sleep?"

Jay Heavner

"No, you and Mom was making too much noise."

John grimaced a little, but in the darkness, the little boy did not notice. John thought all the kids were asleep, but it appeared he was wrong.

The little boy said, "You weren't hurting Mom, were you? She sounded like she was in pain."

John knew they'd been caught, and he had to tell the little boy something his five-year-old mind would understand. "Billy, I'd never hurt your Mom. I love her more than life itself. She's the best thing that ever happened to me." He paused, "sometimes when mommies and daddies play, they may make a lot of noise, but they're just having fun, understand?"

Billy nodded his head, covered in auburn hair. "Daddy," he said. "When you and mommy play, could you play quieter like you sometimes tell us kids? It's hard to sleep with you all playing so loudly."

John said he would try, and the little boy curled up next to him. John put his arm around the small boy who was soon asleep again. When the boy began to snore, his dad picked him up carefully and gently and carried him back into the cabin. He laid him down next to his mother. It would not be the first time one or several of the children would be found in their parent's bed in the morning.

But that was yesterday, and it seemed a lifetime had gone by since then. He looked at the funeral pyre prepared for old Injun Joe. The first day John had seen the old Indian, he'd taken pity on the poor old gray-haired man carrying a haversack with two books in it. A bunch of the boys was making fun of the sick little man and his books. Redskins were too dumb to read, they said, but John knew many whites could not either. John watched for a while but grew tired of the strong tormenting the weak. He separated them and remembered the laughter as he did. John said he would see the old Indian got well, and then he could go on his way. Didn't he know they said the only good Indian was a dead one? He'd slit their throats while they slept, but John ignored them. Over the years, he had developed some empathy for the native population, which had been here before the white man. He remembered how the English pushed around the Scots and Irish in the old world, and he had been a Scot. They just wanted to be left alone and live their lives as they always had for hundreds of years, but even in Scotland, there had been wars and feuds among the various tribes and clans. Either way, there no going back to the way it had been.

John took the sick Indian to his home, and he stayed in the barn with the animals. Jenny was not sure she wanted him around and wondered where they would get extra food. There was little to spare in this growing family. John told her it would be until he got well and was able to travel. After two weeks on the mend, Injun Joe surprised them one day when he came out of the woods with a large doe on his back he killed. They were shocked when he spoke to them in fluent English. "I brought you venison, and it shall feed us for many days. We will make a coat from its skin."

"Where did you learn to speak English... and so good? Why didn't you tell us you could speak our language?" asked John.

The old Indian said, "When I was a young man, I fought a white man who was on our hunting grounds. He was a strong man, and we fought hard and long, but I was a little stronger. I got on top of him and had a knife to run in him. He tried to hold me off, but the knife got closer and closer to his neck. His frightened eyes looked into mine, and he said in my language, 'Please, don't kill me.' I did not think it possible a white man could master our tongue, but here he was talking to me. I let him up, and we became friends. He taught me many things. Why did I not tell you I could speak your language? I had to learn if I could trust you," and then he smiled.

John was glad Injun Joe wanted to stay. He chose to bed down in the barn loft. Any place else was too confining, he said. Often in the cool of the evening, Injun Joe would tell stories of his life to the family. He came from a tribe far to the west where gray eyes and hair like his were common, but all were now dead from smallpox. Only he remained. He owed his life to the white man who knew that a person who got the irritating disease from a cow or rodent would never get the deadly smallpox. Injun Joe had touched a prairie dog with the pox, developed minor sores, but had been unaffected by the often fatal disease that decimated his tribe. Injun Joe had tried to convince the chiefs of the white man's magic medicine, but they did not believe having been tricked so often by the white men, and so all but Injun Joe had died. He showed John how to scratch himself, get the nuisance pox and not the deadly smallpox. John did this to all of his family, and when the pox raged through the area, not one of them got the disease.

The white man named Smyth taught Injun Joe to read English, and he loved the way books could take his mind everywhere. With this knowledge, Injun Joe found he no longer fit in the Indian world, nor in the white world either, so he traveled with Smyth. Smyth lived with his Indian wife in a neighboring village of Injun Joe's tribe before he had encountered him. It was there he learned Injun Joe's tongue. Smyth's wife had died in childbirth, and the devastated man left the tribe. Shortly afterward, Injun Joe encountered the white man. Smyth had big dreams of seeing the world, and Injun Joe caught his traveling fever. The two men traveled west and saw sights no man could believe. The snow-covered mountains touched the skies and buffalo herds made the ground shake from their feet. A great river filled with fish that jumped into the local native's baskets led to a vast and cold ocean. In another place, water spouted from the earth hundreds of feet into the air, and muddy ground boiled. John wondered at some of his stories, but he had never known Injun Joe to be less than honest around him. Injun Joe was on his way to see the eastern ocean when John had found him.

They asked Injun Joe what his tribal name was. He politely smiled and told them no white man, but Smyth had been able to pronounce it. He showed the Phares children how to hunt and how to fight like an Indian. Jasmine, he said, even though she was still a young girl, had the heart of a warrior. She had always been a spunky child, and Injun Joe brought out that inner strength.

And now he was dead, but because of him, the family was alive. John had left for town yesterday morn at dawn for supplies. The men were hiding and watching when John left. They struck the house as the family was waking. The two men quickly overpowered Jenny, tied her hands, and went through the cabin looking for anything of value. Satisfied they had found all worth taking, they set their eyes on Jenny, and their thoughts were pure evil. The biggest one grabbed her and tried to force himself on her, but she managed to slip away. The story she told John went something like this.

Jenny pleaded with the men, "Please, don't do this to me. Please don't."

"There's no one here to stop us, and you're some fine lookin' woman flesh. This should be fun," the biggest one said.

Jenny could see there was no talking them out of their evil. "Please," she pleaded. "Not here in front of the children. If you must do this, at least take me to the barn so my children won't see this."

The big one said, "You know. She's right. That hay should make a good bed. Okay, wench, let's go. I feel myself rising to the occasion," and then he gave a cruel laugh.

The small man laughed too and grabbed Jasmine, who squealed. "And I think I shall enjoy this young thing for the first time."

"We'll have our fun and then kill 'em all, no witnesses," said the big man

"No, don't," shouted Jenny, but it did no good as the two men dragged them to the barn.

In the barn, the big man began to tear at Jenny's dress.

"EEEYYAAAHHH!!" Jenny heard as Injun Joe leaped from the loft in the barn. He landed hard on the big man's back and sank his 16-inch long knife down the side of his neck next to the man's collar bone, and it went in to the handle.

Before Injun Joe could recover, the second man stuck his blade into his back.

"EEEYYAAHHH!!" filled the barn again, and the second man screamed. Jasmine had grabbed a wooden pitch fork and run it in his back below the ribs. Four sharp wooden forks stuck out the front. He painfully turned his head and looked into her eyes.

"EEEYYAAHHH!!" she shouted again and looked coldly at him. "No man, but my husband shall have my maidenhead, and no man, no man, shall ever bugger me."

When John returned, he found the three dead men. Jenny was crying hysterically, and Jasmine was trying to calm her. The rest of the children hid in the cabin. He calmed Jenny and sent the oldest boy for the town constable. They returned quickly, and Jasmine told the lawman what had happened. He said it looked like justice had been done and to dispose of the bodies anyway John saw fit. With the constable's help, he put them in his wagon and took them up into the woods. There he dumped each man on an anthill as large as a new grave. The ants would make quick work of them. It was better than they deserved.

***

It was now mid-morning, and the sun shined at a 45-degree angle. The family gathered around the large woodpile where Injun Joe's body lay on top. His eyes were closed, but he faced the rising sun and the distant ocean he would never see. It was quiet as the older members of the family thought how Injun Joe had affected their lives. Little Billy tugged on his father's breeches. "Daddy, aren't you suppose to say something before we send him off to God?"

"Yes, son. I guess you're right." He cleared his throat. "Dear Lord above. We're here today to honor a good man. I don't even know his real name, but You do. He saved my family, and I own him so much. Would you tell him, 'Thanks' please? There is no way I could ever repay him. I know he believed in a Great Spirit who created all. Today may his soul soar like an eagle up to you and land in the hollow of your hand. Amen."

Each of the family, even the smallest, echoed an "Amen."

John lit the fire, and a roaring inferno soon consumed the old Indian. The fire was hot, and the family backed away. They stood hugging together at a safe distance. Tears ran down their faces, even John's. A great man was going home. John hoped he could be as honorable as this old Indian was in life and death. Greater love hath no man than he would lay down his life for another.

Chapter 12

Spring 1774

It was late afternoon when John Phares saw the red-headed stranger come riding up to his farm. He wore a tri-cornered hat and was dressed warmly against the chill. The weather was not favorable for travel. The first warming breezes of spring were late arriving. It would be another month before the leaves would appear. The man rode closer, and John recognized him.

"Why, Mr. Washington. It's a pleasure to see you. What brings you to these parts?"

Washington responded from high on his horse. "I'm well, thank God. I hope the sicknesses I've had are behind me." He dismounted. "I'm in the area on business. Change is in the air, and there's much to do. Would it be possible to lodge here for the night? I want to discuss some matters with you. Finding someone I can trust and be candid with is difficult these days."

"Mr. Washington, you know you're always welcome here."

"Please, we've known each other for so long. I would much prefer it if you called me George. Let's put the horse in the barn and then discuss some items of importance." Two of John's children followed them to the barn. They put the horse in a stall and gave the gelding some of last season's hay. The children pick up brushes and gently groomed the horse.

Washington said, "John, you and your family have shown me nothing but kindness ever since I have known you. Jenny has been a wife every man dreams of having and look at your children. My, how they've grown. I guess it won't be long before you'll be a grandpa."

"Well, George," he hesitated, "it will take a while to get used to calling you George and not your last name with a title in front of it. My oldest is of marrying age, but she is a headstrong young woman. It'll take a special man to win her heart, and she knows her papa loves her too much to marry her off to the first suitor that shows up. She's different. She may be a girl, but she can outrun and hold her own against men her size and bigger. Any man who underestimates that filly will get a surprise real quick. I don't know what the future has in store for her, but I believe her life will be different from most women here on the frontier."

"So true, each time I see her, she grows bigger and stronger. The good Lord above has blessed you with quite a family."

"Yes, He has. The youngin's take care of the horse. The missus has supper cooking. Why don't we head for the porch and talk about whatever is on your mind."

"That would be fine, but let's save the serious items until after we've eaten. Some things are better discussed on a full stomach. I have some excellent tobacco with me that was raised on my plantation. Would you care for some?"

John's ears perked up. Good tidewater tobacco was prized highly on the frontier. "Excellent idea. First, we have a smoke, then a good meal, and later get down to business. I like your line of thinking. George, as we're friends, I can say this, people say you're not the quickest thinker, but you have the ability to take a problem apart and come to a precise plan of action. I hope you are not offended by my bluntness."

Washington cringed slightly and smiled. At one time, his temper would have his mouth spewing something he'd later regret, but he'd learned, for the most part, to keep it in check. "Yes, I have heard this said about me. We grow old so soon… and smart so late. What I have to discuss will need bluntness and candor, but must remain confidential."

The two men walked to the porch, and George sat on the crude bench. John checked with Jenny on the supper. The kids were helping, and it would be ready soon. The tobacco was every bit as smooth as John remembered the excellent, lowland product. They made small talk about the weather and how things were changing ever so fast. Soon they were called to a grand supper--salted pork, cornbread, some dried apples, and boiled skunk cabbage. John asked his guest to bless the meal. Washington did and also asked for the good Lord's blessing upon this household. He received a big Amen from all sitting at the table John had made during a cold winter long ago. The meal was delicious, though it was devoured by the hungry people; Jenny was certain she was the only one to noticed how it tasted.

Jenny and the kids cleaned up the table and dishes afterward, and the men retreated to the porch. "That was a mighty fine meal, John. It's a wonder with cooking like that you aren't a stout man."

John chuckled. "If my body really reflected how good my wife's cooking has been, I would be as wide as I am tall. The ladies have ways of taking care of us menfolk."

Washington's eyebrows raised, and he now also chuckled. "How right you are. How right you are," he repeated. "As I said, I have some important news and business I must share with you. The times are a changing. There's talk of rebellion against the British mainly in the New England area, but there are pockets everywhere in the colonies. The die has been cast, and I fear there is no turning back. Various people have quietly asked me to lead an army against the Motherland. I'd hoped it would not come to this, but the actions of the Crown are only making matters worse instead of better. I believe war is on the horizon, and it's not something to rush into. Many will die, and there will be much destruction. Once it starts, no one can be sure of the outcome. I've been inspecting the western frontier for defense. If war comes, I fear the British will rally the Indians against us. They will see the British as the lesser of two evils."

"You've seen how it goes. The Crown ignored the threat from the French in the Ohio region years ago. When they pushed our forces out, the Indians saw them as the stronger and sided with them. Some wavered. You well know what happened after Braddock's defeat. We lost all Indian support, and many settlers on the frontier died."

"Some of this present situation can be traced back to that bullheaded Englishman General Braddock. If he had only listened and not been so headstrong, things might have been different."

"What do you mean?" asked John.

"Now, don't get me wrong," said George Washington. "I greatly appreciated what he did for me by allowing me to be his aide. I treasure his sash he gave me, but his actions have had great consequences. He was pompous and ham-handed. He dismissed the Colonial Forces and his Indians allies as unimportant and incompetent. Look where it got him, dead." George paused for effect. "The Scotsman General Forbes had his own ideas on how things should be done, some of what I did not agree with, but he learned from Braddock's mistakes and was able to overcome the French. Braddock's defeat gave the Indians hope of pushing back our settler's advances, and many of them died needlessly. Also, it made the King's forces look poorly in the colonial's eyes. They were no longer our saviors, but just another army that could be defeated. If Braddock had been effective, the Crown would see no need to impose the taxes and restrictions many here view as dictatorial. We are free men equal to them, not pawns to be pushed around."

The two men sat silently as the darkness came. Only the burning tobacco in the pipes penetrated the night, and the smoke kept the mosquitoes at bay. They could barely see each other. After a long pause, John Phares spoke. "So, where do we go from here?"

Washington responded. "Thank you for listening to my rants and frustration. You were there. You knew." He stopped and started again. "There're two matters where you can possibly help me. War with the British is coming quickly, and we must prepare. The frontier is still vulnerable to attacks from the Indians of Ohio, further west and Canada. The British will stir them up against us just like the French did. Yesterday's enemy may be today's ally. I need forces for the war starting in New England now, but I also need men to stay behind on the frontier to guard our back door against invaders. I want you to stay and do what you can in the western mountains of Virginia and neighboring Pennsylvania."

John said, "Yes, I can understand the logic in that, and the second matter is?"

Washington hesitated, "It's something I'm not sure how to address. After Braddock's defeat, his payroll is believed to have disappeared. Some say Dunbar had it with his forces at the rear, and it was never lost. Others say it was lost at the Battle of the Monongahela and is still lost, or the French have it and are not talking. Still, others say it was buried somewhere along the Youghiogheny River. I tend to believe that report. Over the years, British officials have approached me for information, but I had little to give. I was so ill as were many on that campaign. I spent more time riding prone in the sick-wagon than on my horse. When I could ride, I needed a pillow under me as my hinder parts were raw from wiping. Only the battle made me forget how rash and tender it was."

John gave a little laugh at that and said, "I think any person can sympathize with you. That condition is a plague on humanity on the frontier. In a way, you were lucky. Many died from that condition."

"How well I know," said Washington. "It's only funny when it's long over, or someone else has it."

John laughed again. "I've been there and know first hand what you speak of."

Washington continued. "Even others believe it was buried in Virginia near Alexandria. The British must know something, or they would not still be looking for it. John, the colonial cause of freedom, is in dire need of money. You were on Braddock's campaign. I'm not asking if you know where it is, but if you did and could see that some comes my way, it would be a great help. Many men on the coast have given large sums privately. Some will lose all they have in the coming war, and that could include me. My home is along the Potomac and within a cannon shot of a passing British warship. If you know anything about getting some of the lost gold payroll into trusted hands, I would be eternally grateful. And as you well know, I can be trusted with a secret."

John sucked on his pipe. In the red glow from its bowl, he could see Washington was looking at him. He nodded his head. "Yes, I've heard the same stories and may know something about it." He said no more, and the two men sat in silence, puffing their pipes. The smoke did an excellent job keeping gnats and mosquitoes away. A whippoorwill cried in the darkness and was answered by another far away. John remembered how the ghostly noise frightened him when he first came to the New World. Only after learning the haunting sound came from a small bird, did his fears left him. The birds continued to call and answer until a wolf howled in the distance. Perhaps tonight, a pack would take down one of the few remaining elk or wapiti as the Shawnee called them. He had not heard one bellowing for many moons.

The night grew chilly, and the two men went inside for the night. John showed Washington a straw tick on the floor where he could sleep. Jenny had prepared for their guest. He could sleep in the crowded, warm cabin and not the barn. Soon the burning embers in the fireplace were the only thing providing light in the one-room filled with snoring people of all sizes.

Early the next morning at dawn, all hands were called to prepare the breakfast, including the visiting Washington. John left to attend to the horses in the nearby barn. When he returned, the food was waiting. All ate a morning meal of eggs, salted ham, bread, and strong coffee. The latter was a luxury few on the frontier could afford. After the meal, John let Jenny and the kids do the cleanup, and he took Washington to the barn. He pointed to a saddlebag on Washington's horse. He said, "I did a little inquiring after all had gone to bed last night. You will find some of what you need for the coming endeavors in the saddlebags. I believe you know what to do with it."

Washington opened the bag, carefully stuck in his hand, and pulled out several coins, gold coins. He looked at John and smiled. "You've always been able to come through for me. Thank you, and a nation still unborn thanks you. And as I said, I can keep a secret." He put his index finger to his closed lips.

Washington climbed onto his horse and was soon off down the slope. At the bottom, he turned and waved. John waved back as did the children on the porch of the cabin. It was then; he noticed Jenny standing behind him. He grimaced and asked, "How long have you been standing there?"

"Long enough," she said. "John, I've known you weren't going for ginseng up in Pennsylvania years ago. At first, I thought you may have another woman or more somewhere, as do some of the long hunters. They're no better than sailors with a girl in every port. But it just didn't add up, and when Boone with his Quaker upbringings showed up with you, I knew I could trust you, though I still wasn't sure what you were doing till some years later. John, I've suspected your gold stash for years now. I knew this farm did not provide for all we had, and you were getting money from somewhere. I listened to your conversation with Washington last night, and it all came together."

"Jenny, you'd make a good spy. I'm kind of glad you know. Let it be our little secret together."

"Okay, and I have a secret for you. In about six months there will be the pitter-patter of little feet around the house again, and I'm not talking of a new dog." She smiled and let the news sink in.

"Jenny, that's wonderful. It looks like I have another reason to stay and guard the home front."

And he did, though no Indians attacked the little growing community around Ashby's old Fort. Fighting with the Indians would be further west along the Ohio and with the bloody British far to the east along the Atlantic. Just the same, John was ready, but other things required his attention during these troubled times.

Chapter 13

1780 in the Indian Village of Chillicothe, Shawnee territory, present-day Ohio

Old Chief Bimino of the Delaware tribe sat warming himself by the fire that spring day. His eyes were clouded, and his body feeble, but his mind was still clear. Age had not affected it like it had his sight and muscles. The visit from the three white men had stirred memories he would have just as soon forgotten. The world would continue on with or without his presence, and men would continue to be greedy and lust for more. They would breed, fight, kill others, and die either from their battles or old age, and then the cycle would continue over and over again.

He hated those who had pushed his tribe west to Ohio from its homelands to the east on the Susquehanna River. His tribe, the Leni Lenape, or the Delaware as the whites called them, and the Shawnee had been forced out by both the stronger native Iroquois Nation and the English. They both wanted what was best for them, and the Delaware and Shawnee tribes were in the way. The two tribes would eventually find refuge here to the west of the Ohio River. This was the way of the world. His tribe had many, many years ago conquered and killed off another tribe and taken their land as their own. Today, all the old man wanted was to live and die in peace and maybe have a little vengeance to those who had wronged him.

He hated the Englishmen in Pennsylvania who had wanted more and more land from them. Especially he hated William Penn's sons involved in the "Walking Purchase." The Indians should have known better than to trust the forked-tongue white men. They agreed the

Delaware would give up the land a walking man could travel in a day and a half and no more. This man did not walk like a normal man, but "walked" with the speed of a deer pursued by wolves. He did not stop to eat or rest and had left their best warriors, witnesses to the treaty, in his dust. Some whites, he had found he could trust over time, but others only gained your trust to cheat and steal from you. How did one tell the difference? It had been better to hate and kill them all.

He was tired and would soon sleep with his father. The young braves would have to adapt to the white's ways or fight them to the death. The whites were too strong.

The English forced the Delaware from the east, and Bimino, known to the whites as Killbuck, had lived among the English settlers in western Pennsylvania and the valleys of the South Branch of the Potomac River in Virginia during the 1740s and 1750s. His tribe knew the area as Wappacomo. A Mr. Peter Casey hired him to track down a runaway slave for a fee. When it came time to collect, the two men quarreled over the payment, and Casey knocked Killbuck down with his cane. How he wished to kill him from that day forward, but never had been able. Casey always managed to slip away. Just the same, many other whites would die from the knowledge he gleaned while living among them. Later, they would find shelter and protection with the Shawnee tribe across the Ohio River.

The French were traders in goods the Indians wanted and needed and did not seem to crave the land as did the English. Like Killbuck, they hated the English, but could they be a powerful enough ally to drive the English back into the sea? He had believed so and thrown his support to them. Many whites had paid in blood for their deeds against him and his people. Killbuck and his warriors had killed the father of one of the men who visited with him. When he heard the names of his visitors, Vincent Williams, Benjamin Peter Casey, and John Phares, he had been surprised, though he had not shown it. It was funny how they wanted to dig up old war stories that had been buried, but yet seek his help in keeping peace with the Americans on the western frontier. They whiskey brought as a gift warmed his body and loosened his tongue. They said they wanted to know it all.

Tell them the history of his tribe and the whites, but Killbuck knew some details should be dealt with carefully.

"I will start my story with the man known as Washington," Killbuck said. "He was a young fool when he attacked the French party when Jumon was killed. I hear he has learned much over the past years of warfare and is now fighting his old allies, the British. If you want me to persuade my people not to join the British in their fight against the Americans, I cannot. I am blind, old, and feeble, and the young braves no longer listen to me."

"I fought the whites in many battles. One, you called the 'Battle of the Trough' near the corn planting grounds of Old Fields. We killed many that day. One group of warriors battled your father, Mr. Williams. He was a brave man." Killbuck thought it best to omit the part about Mr. Williams killing five warriors before he died, and the Indians quartered his body and left his head on a pike.

"Mr. Ben Casey, I have no quarrel with you, but I would kill your father, Peter, today if I could. He refused to pay me for my retrieving a runaway slave and hit me with his cane. You can pay me his debt of 8 shillings, and all will be forgiven," but Killbuck did not expect to be paid despite his offer.

"General Braddock died near the forks of the Ohio, and we thought victory was ours if we continued to push the British and Colonials back to the eastern sea. We did for two years running, but a few settlers held on."

"And Mr. Phares, many times during the war when you were Washington's messenger, we wanted to kill you, but you managed to slip away. I congratulate you on keeping your scalp. Many wanted to take it. You were at the battle on the Cacapon River near Fort Edwards. You remember, we killed the commander Mercer and wounded Daniel Morgan, but you escaped untouched."

John Phares thought of the letters he carried to Governor Dinwiddie and the Virginia Assembly from Colonel Washington, pleading for help in countering the savage's attacks on the frontier. Little did they understand the situation, and aid was long in coming and nowhere adequate.

Killbuck continued, "After a long and hard winter, we came again for battle in the year you know as 1758. We attacked the stockade called Fort Upper Tract destroying it, killed many, and took prisoners. The next day, we went over the mountains and trapped the whites in their round stockade they called Fort Seybert. A few fought bravely, but a foolish old man opened the gate when we promised no harm to those inside. We kept our promise, just like the whites taught us to trust theirs. We killed all we had no use for with the tomahawk, about 20, and carried off the rest with some items of value. And then we burned the fort. The settlers had much gold coin we placed in a pot and made them carry. It had little value to us, but the French treasured it greatly, and we could trade it for much goods. But it is heavy. We feared pursuit, and it slowed us down. We buried it among rocks and hoped to go back later to retrieve it, but could not. Forbes victory at the forks of the Ohio River would knock the fight out of our allies, the French."

Killbuck took another long swig from the whiskey bottle, swallowed, and began speaking again after a short pause. "A young white boy named Nicholas was with me in a canoe as we crossed a great river, and I saw him eyeing some distant ducks. I asked, is your eyesight good?

"He answered quickly, 'About as good as common.'

"My next question scared him, 'Did you shoot my two men from the fort?' He trembled, and I order him to speak. The boy was brave, and I liked that, but I did not let him see this at first.

"'Yes,' he said, 'and I know I hit them.'

"How did you know you hit them? What evidence did you have of this?" I asked.

"'The one I shot in the head, and I saw his head feathers floating in the stream water, and the other screamed out in pain when I shot him in the hip,' the boy said.

"Both men died," said Killbuck.

"'And I would have killed you, too, if the old man who let you in the fort had not pushed my gun barrel way as I tried to fire on you,'" the boy continued.

A cruel smile came to Killbuck's ugly face. "You are a brave boy. You did right in shooting as you did. We were your enemy. The tribe will adopt you, and you will become one of us. Then you will use that gun to kill the whites who will be your enemy."

"We traveled on to the village at Chillicothe. Later that year, we learned of British General Forbes's victory over the French at the forks of the Ohio. A short-lived peace came to the land and Nicholas, and numerous other captured white children were returned. Many did not want to go but were forced to do so. Some escaped and returned to us."

He paused, "I am out of whiskey, but I have one more thing to tell, I think will interest you." He stopped talking and waited. The three men looked at each other puzzled until John realized what Killbuck wanted. He pulled a bottle of whiskey from his haversack and placed it in the Indian's hand.

Killbuck smiled slightly. He took a drink, swallowed, and his smile became thoughtful. He spoke, "I have found a few things to be true in my life. One is that a man who says he's never been scared is either a liar or has never done anything or been anywhere. Two, gold and trouble usually come as a pair. When gold comes into a man's thinking, common sense goes away. Gold is a hard-found thing and even harder to keep. A man usually finds it when he is not looking."

The three men looked at each other surprised and puzzled. John shifted uneasily.

"We had a young woman here in the village who was captured from the Cherokee," Killbuck said. "She spoke English and Cherokee already and quickly learned our language and also French. She was unusually smart. She was sold to a French trader who later took her as his wife.

"At that time, my sight and hearing were still very good. The Indians from several tribes returned to camp with booty from raids. The warriors traded their gold coins for bottles of whiskey, and the Frenchman was pleased with this deal. The braves did not know the value of what they had and sold much too cheap. That seems the way it has always been between the whites and Indians. One gold piece was on a necklace he gave to the woman. I overheard the Frenchman tell her he believed it part of Braddock's lost gold payroll, and he wanted it for his own. I think gold is a curse and that is why I tell you this. I think many more white men will die seeking it, more than all tribes of the Indians could ever kill. Happy hunting." He paused for effect. " Now, I am tired, and I wish you to go before the whiskey makes me forget I am old and blind and wish to kill you."

The three men knew it was best to say nothing. They quickly rose and walked from the campfire where Killbuck sat drinking the whiskey. Killbuck was right. Gold and trouble came as a pair. Gold clouded a man's thinking. Killbuck knew he had opened a Pandora's box, and the three men had better beware. They would not be the last to deal with this snare.

Jay Heavner

Chapter 14

June 1975

It was only after Tom had become a father himself, that he fully appreciated all his dad had done for him. Tom's mother died young from cancer, and his dad became both mother and father to him. Life on the hard-scrabble farm had never been easy. It seemed no matter how hard you worked; there was never enough money, so Tom's dad did what many men in his situation had to do; they drove a school bus for the county to supplement their income. Tom should have gone to school in Ridgeley or Wiley Ford, but his father hadn't wanted him standing alone along WV Route 28 waiting for a bus. He rode his dad's bus to the Short Gap School and later to Fort Ashby High. No questions had been asked about the correct school district for him when he started, and once in, the subject never came up.

Tom often wondered why his dad never remarried. He guessed he had been too busy with the farm, his work and raising Tom, and maybe the right woman had never come along. He'd never heard his dad say an unkind word about his mother, who Tom could hardly remember. He'd been so young when she died. She must have been some woman.

His dad had done a great job raising him. It was not that Tom was perfect by any means, but his dad just seemed to know what needed to be done. Tom had been pretty hard-headed and stubborn as a kid. It was only later he understood his dad's lament, "Guess you're blessed with children just like you." His dad had been like him and sometimes had to learn the hard way, too.

Tom's dad fixed up his old pickup truck with a camper on the back. When he had time, his dad would take him to places usually within 150 miles distance of home. They'd been to the nation's capital several times and nearby national and state parks, but what they enjoyed most was camping, fishing, and canoeing. For canoeing, they floated on nearby rivers and creeks. The North Branch of the Potomac at that time was too polluted with industrial discharge, acid mine drainage, and sewage for recreation. A great job of cleanup was being done now, and hopefully soon, it would be clean enough to use, but in the 1950s and 60s, tributaries of the South Branch were usually the place to go. Patterson Creek was small but close. They made certain there was ample water before they would go as there wasn't always. They floated from the Route 46 Bridge all the way to the low water bridge near the little town of Patterson Creek. The stretch from Fort Ashby to the low water bridge was especially fun on a hot summer's day, but portage was required around the old rock dam's remains and the ford where the creek ran wide and low.

They canoed and camped the South Branch from Moorefield to Millison's Mill near Springfield. The first time Tom had ever seen marijuana was along that stretch. His dad told him what the curious tall Christmas tree-shaped weed was. The US Navy had planted it as a source of hemp for rope during WW II. They were concerned the Japanese would cut off the supply from Southeast Asia, mainly the Philippians. He heard some people had tried to smoke it and get high, but only succeeded in burning their lungs and throats from the smoke. Whether you could get high on it or not, the law looked at it as illegal drugs and would arrest you for possession. Tom and his dad just looked at the tall, dark weed, but never picked.

The trip through the Trough was something Tom would never forget. Tom's dad rented a canoe from the Trough General Store, south of Romney. They parked behind the store, and the business owner, a kindly young man, transported them and the canoe to the put-in place north of Moorefield, WV. The water was clear and cool that morning. He warned them about a rock ledge in the river they needed to avoid about 500 feet before the high railroad bridge. The ledge had swamped many a canoe, and they were grateful for the advice. Once past the bridge, civilization ended except for the railroad on the left-hand side that was not often visible. The river ran through a 1,000 foot deep cleft between two steep mountains. Long, deep pools with some minor rapids between them made for a leisurely float if you were careful. Some massive rocks nearly rose to the surface, and you better miss them. In the deep pools, Tom and his dad would occasionally see huge fish darting for cover in the dark water as they passed.

They saw at least forty Canadian geese swimming by one at a time and several bald eagles in different trees watched them and waiting to make a meal of an unsuspecting fish. The deer they saw were curious but ran for cover in the thick brush as they passed. It was so quiet and still. You could almost feel the presence of men like George Washington or the Indian Chief Killbuck who had traveled this area many times. A crashing on the hillside startled the men, but they could not see what caused a tree to fall. Was it gravity pulling down a rotten old, dead tree, or maybe a bear scratching at it for grubs to eat? Tom's dad had joked it may be a yayhoo, but Tom had never heard of a beast named this. His dad explained that the Rockies had Big Foot, Florida had its swamp ape and in West Virginia, the creature was called a yayhoo. He knew of men who claimed to see them in remote areas of the state, and they usually had a degree of fear in their voice as the story unfolded. Whatever it was that day, it did not hang around for inspection, which was okay with them. They had a great and memorable day.

Tom had taken all his sons on this canoe trip when they were growing up, and he hoped to do the same with Joann and his stepdaughter Miriah. Tom told numerous people about the fun on the river. Some took the river ride, and all had liked it except for one couple who were caught in a driving summer thunderstorm. Life happens.

Tom could not remember his father's parents. They passed when he was young. His dad had been a veteran of WW II, serving with

General Patton in Europe. Only years later did certain things he had heard his dad say and do make sense.

His dad always had an interest in flying. They'd go to the nearby Cumberland Airport in Wiley Ford and watch the planes take off. He knew some of the pilots of the small aircraft and would occasionally when he had a few extra bucks, which wasn't often, talk the pilots into letting Tom and him ride along on the local flights. He'd help out when they had the auto races at the airport. Tom figured this was why he knew so many of the people. At one of the events, his dad won a raffle for a glider flight sponsored by the Cumberland Soaring Club, and Saturday's weather made it perfect conditions to soar. They arrived at the airport early in the morning and parked near the hangar as instructed. The planes and gliders were out on the runways and ready to go.

He remembered his father talking to the officials and them pointing to their glider, and it was a big one, a Schweitzer 2-32. They walked to the plane, and his father introduced them to a strikingly handsome man a little over 6 feet tall. He had piercing eyes and wavy hair with streaks of gray and said his name was Werner von Braun. Only years later did Tom understood the tense conversation in the glider between the two men.

The three of them climbed into the glider, and in a few minutes, the tow plane pulled them high up in the air over the airport and set them free. Air dropped off Allegheny Front from the nearly 3,000 foot high Big Savage Mountain into the much lower Potomac River Valley and ran into Knobley Mountain. This created an uplift in the atmosphere and made it a perfect place for soaring.

The two adults chatted about the weather as the glider gained altitude over the Cumberland area. For Tom, it was exciting and somewhat frightening, too. He felt like a god looking down on the earth from on high but was also scary, this being his first time aloft. From this altitude, he could see the whole of Cumberland and much of the surrounding area, including the old farm he called home. What happened next was something he'd not understand until years later. His dad struck up a conversation with the pilot.

Jay Heavner

"So Mr. von Braun, I saw you on the news and know you are now working for NASA, but what brings you to the Cumberland, Maryland area?"

He replied in his excellent English that still had a mild German accent, "Oh, a number of things. NASA wants me to pound the flesh, you know, shake a lot of hands and do some much-needed PR work. I'm speaking at Keyser High School and various other places in the area. NASA wants me to drum up support for the space program. Congress has a way of being stingy with funding and the more calls the representatives get from the people back home, the better our budget will be in space exploration."

He went on, "Just between you and me; I'm hedging my bets, too. If we don't receive the funding, I may need another job. Various companies have contacted me, and I'm looking at options. And there is this too, soaring. I discovered this place while job hunting and speaking. I loved to do this when I was in Germany. Up here, it's so relaxing. You can forget your problems and all the evil things that can happen down on the ground. It's so peaceful in a glider with just the wind currents to hold you."

Tom's dad asked, "Do you spend much time on Cape Canaveral?"

"I go there regularly. It's a beautiful area, but the mosquitoes can carry you away at times."

"Do you know of a place down there called Canaveral Flats? It's between Titusville and Cocoa."

Von Braun turned around and spoke, "I can't say the name Canaveral Flats rings a bell, but Titusville and Cocoa do. We often fly into the Tico Airport in Titusville or other times use the skid strip at the Cape Canaveral facility. I must have flown over it at one time."

"My cousin married a guy whose brother came into some money somehow, and he bought a big chunk of raw land in the area they call Canaveral Flats. He's been cutting roads through the palmettos and selling lots, mainly to people from up here in the mountains. A goodly number have moved down there, and some are using it as an escape from the winter cold. I guess with the space race; jobs are available in Brevard County. He's got no restrictions on the land use, so I hear the place can be kind of tacky with old trailers and such, but that was the way he wanted it; just common salt of the earth people. He's got no use for people who look down their noses at you and think they're somehow better because they got more money."

"Yes," von Braun said. "I've been around people such as that. There should be a place for everyone."

"He talked one of my cousins, Bill Kenney, who'd been a Mineral County Deputy, into coming down a time ago and he's now the head of the police department in Canaveral Flats. I heard from him a while back. He said it was mostly peaceful, but occasionally they have some trouble just like anyplace else."

Von Braun chuckled, "Ah yes, West Virginia. It's all relative. I would fit right in."

Tom's dad laughed at that too, but he became serious. "Mr. von Braun, what did you do in the war? I was a soldier with General Patton."

Von Braun paused, inhaled, and let out a deep breath. "That is an easy, but yet a hard question. I served my nation in the best way I knew how, but sometimes I've wondered if I, we were not all pawns in a bigger game. You have an expression here, 'Can't see the forest for the trees,' I believe it is."

"I was one of the men who liberated the underground concentration camp at Mittelbau-Dora, where rockets were made."

Von Braun said nothing for a moment. "One of your greatest soldiers, Robert E. Lee, once said, 'It is well that war is so terrible - otherwise we would grow too fond of it.' Horrible things are done in war. People turn on people. I myself was arrested by the Gestapo and feared for my life. Sir Winston Churchill also noted, 'Never, never, never believe any war will be smooth and easy, or that anyone who embarks on the strange voyage can measure the tides and hurricanes he will encounter. The statesman who yields to war fever must realize that once the signal is given, he is no longer the master of policy but the slave of unforeseeable and uncontrollable events.' There have been times I wonder if we are not all slaves."

"I believe you've thought much on this matter since the Great War," said Tom's dad. Von Braun nodded. "Mr. von Braun, have you ever heard of Operation Paper Clip?"

Tom could see von Braun cringe slightly at the mention of Operation Paper Clip.

Von Braun asked, "How do you know that name? It is supposed to be a secret."

Tom's dad said, "I was part of that too. I was only a clerk who read and shuffled papers for the brass, but I saw much I did not like. Many crimes were swept under the rug. They said it all involved national security, but I wondered at the wisdom of some in charge. I feared it could someday come back to bite us."

"You are a surprise, Mr. Kenney. Never would I have thought we would talk about this when I first saw you. Mr. Kenney, you are right. Although none of the German scientists brought over here were totally guilt-free, remember what I now say because I will not repeat it again. There were and still are wolves among the sheep. I can say no more."

No one spoke for a long while in the glider. Each seemed to be lost in his thoughts. Von Braun skillfully flew the airship on the thermals. Even to Tom's untrained eyes, he could see Von Braun knew what he was doing and was used to being in control. They were high above the airport at Wiley Ford, and Tom could see his home, the mountain behind it with the old field in the cove on top, and much of the area. The small towns of Patterson Creek and Oldtown downriver and Fort Ashby were visible also. Someday again, he hoped to do this. Though you had to depend on the wind, Tom sensed a freedom hard to describe. They flew about another hour with little more than polite conversation before returning to terra firma. It was a day Tom would never forget for several reasons.

***

June 1975 at the Kenney farm at Short Gap, WV.

That Saturday started out like many other weekends at the old farmhouse. Tom and Sarah had their hands full caring for the toddler Bryan and Tom's dad, whose Parkinson's Disease robbed him of his mobility, but not his mental function. Though he had trouble getting around without assistance and speaking, his mind was still sharp. And to make it more interesting, Sarah was pregnant with their second child. Tom was checking on the steer they raised for beef when the shadow went over him. *What was that?* He thought. *That's way too big for a buzzard.* Sarah came running around the house, and she was excited. "Tom, a small plane just crashed up on the mountain top! You need to get up there and see what happened. Someone may need help. I'll call the Fire Department, but it may be a while before they can get here and up there. Do what you can to help the people in the plane."

Tom said he would. He grabbed a backpack, a walkie-talkie, a first aid kit, and his 9mm handgun he may need for some dealing with some coyotes he had seen lately. He headed up the steep mountain road behind the house as swiftly as he could. He saw evidence of wildlife activity. Twice he noted deer droppings and a small tree with bark missing. A buck used it for rubbing the velvet off his antlers.

It took him at least 15 minutes to arrive at the crash site in the field on the mountain top cove. The glider was reasonably intact except for damage to the right-wing, which hit a tree. A grey-haired man sat on a rock with his back to Tom. As Tom walked closer, he could hear him say, *"Bose menschen ungestraft bleiden, bose menschen ungestraft bleiden,"* over and over. Tom looked at the man who seemed in a daze. A small trickle of blood ran from a goose egg lump on his forehead. *"Bose menschen ungestraft bleiden,"* he kept repeating.

Tom faced the man and asked, "Are you okay?"

He looked at Tom and repeated, *"Bose menschen ungestraft bleiden."*

"What do you mean?" asked Tom. He wondered if the hit to the head had knocked the man silly. "Are you okay?"

The gray-haired man who looked to be mid-60s said, "The wind just died, but I am okay. What do I mean, *'Bose menschen ungestraft bleiden?'* It means evil men go unpunished. We have done so much evil that even today, it follows us. I am so glad God can forgive all. Man cannot."

Tom looked at the man carefully and said, "Hey, I know you. We've met before. You're Werner von Braun."

Surprise came to the man's eyes. "You look familiar, but I can't place you. When did we meet?"

"It was about 10- 15 years ago when I was a teen. My dad won a raffle for a glider ride at the Cumberland Airport. We went soaring with you. You crashed on our farm today." Von Braun studied Tom. "I'm Tom, Tom Kenney. I remember you and my dad discussing WW II and something called Operation Paper Clip."

"Yes, yes, now I remember that day. Your father is a noble man. I trust he is well."

"My father's near here, but he's crippled up with Parkinson's disease. How's your head?"

"My head hurts," he said as he wiped the blood away from his head and then stood. "I will survive this, but my days on this earth are coming to an end. The doctors told me a month ago I have pancreatic cancer and I should get my affairs in order. I made my peace with God years ago, and I purchased a grave plot in Alexandria last week. You know who I am. I have been engaged in Germany's and America's race to get into the skies and space since the beginning, and I want Psalms 19:1 on my grave marker; 'The heavens declare the Glory of the Lord and the firmaments show His handiwork.' That will be my testimony when I am gone."

Tom said nothing for a moment. Von Braun was not seriously hurt, he believed. He was coherent, and his legs were steady. The walkie-talkie Tom had cracked. It was Sarah speaking, "Tom, how are things up there? The Short Gap Fire Department has arrived. Should they hurry up there, or is it too late?"

"It's okay. I'm with the pilot here. He has a lump on his head, but he's up, and we'll walk down to them. The glider's gonna need some help getting off the mountain, but overall it's not in bad shape.

Got a busted up wing, but it can be fixed. We'll see you soon. Don't let the volunteers leave till they've taken a look at the pilot."

"Will do, see you soon. Out."

Tom looked at von Braun, who spoke, "Thank you for not telling them who I am. I would like to keep this quiet, and I would like to talk to your father privately if that would be possible."

"I think my father would like to talk with you too, but I don't know if you're gonna keep a lid on this. You're famous, and you've been in the news so much. One more story won't hurt."

"Perhaps you're right. There are many things in our lives we cannot control," and as an afterthought, he added, "and there are many we can."

The two men walked down the steep mountain road and were greeted by Nacho, the donkey who brayed loudly. "Nacho," Tom said. "You'll wake the dead with that noise."

"Please, Mr. Kenney, after my recent brush with the grim reaper, I am happy to hear his bellowing." He walked over to the fence and began to stroke the animal's head. Von Braun produced an apple from his pocket and fed it to Nacho. "You have a very intelligent creature here Mr. Kenney, and one who thinks he is a big watchdog."

"That he is," said Tom. "I think we had better get goin'. We can't keep the emergency responders waiting."

"Yes, you're right." He looked at the donkey and said, "Mr. Nacho, it is a pleasure to have met such as fine ass as you."

The donkey perked up at the mention of his name, and the two men walked to the house where the EMTs were waiting. They gave von Braun a quick examination, but he assured them he was fine. They wanted to take him to the hospital to have his head x-rayed, but he refused any of their suggestions, so they left.

Von Braun asked to use the house phone. He made a call to the Soaring Club and gave them an update on what happened. They'd send a car to pick him up and made arrangements with the Kenneys to retrieve the aircraft on the mountain later. After the call, Tom took von Braun to see his father on the porch. They recognized each other and asked Tom to leave. They wished to speak in private.

Jay Heavner

They spoke for twenty minutes, and a car pulled into Tom's driveway. It was a man from the Soaring Club. Von Braun shouted from the porch for the driver to please wait. He would be along soon. When they were done, von Braun walked back into the house and found Tom at the table.

"Done so soon?" asked Tom.

"Yes, we are done. We are like two old warriors. We no longer want to fight our past demons and wish to be at peace with each other."

"It's a good thing when a man can make peace with himself and others," said Tom. 'You're welcome to return here."

"Thank you for your help today, Mr. Tom Kenney. I would like that, but my time grows short, and I know not if I will have many tomorrows. I must leave. Again, thank you for your kindness." He left the house and walked toward the waiting car. "Oh, one more thing I need to tell someone. Not all the men from Germany who your government brought here are sheep. Some are still wolves dressed in sheep's skin. Beware."

He said no more, got in the car, and waved goodbye as they drove off. It would be many years before Tom would understand von Braun's warning.

Chapter 15

The day started early for Tom. His son Doug called him the night before and told him of a situation. Their young driver whose wife had recently had their first child called in late Sunday to say he wouldn't be in Monday. The child was sick and needed to be hospitalized. They would be with the doctors and the young child all day Monday, maybe longer.

Tom rose early, leaving his wife Joann in bed still in dreamland. He had a bowl of muesli with blueberries, some Florida's Natural Brand orange juice, two pieces of kielbasa, a cup of coffee, (Chock Full 'O Nuts of course), and read a devotional article on hardship in *Our Daily Bread*. Its underlying theme was given a lemon, make lemonade. He finished his breakfast, cleared the table of dishes, rinsed, and placed them in the dishwasher. Tom grabbed a jacket to protect him from the cold, brisk fall weather. The first rays of the sun were coming up in the east just over Patterson Creek Ridge. Soon Ole Sol would bathe the land with sunlight. It had been dry, and that made conditions perfect for the tourists coming to see the colored leaves. *This will make an excellent year for all the festivals*. Those people will really have a great turnout if it doesn't turn too cold and rainy. It meant extra business for him.

People needed bottled water at these events, and he was okay with selling his quality product to them. The more word got out about his Knobley Mountain Bottled Water, the better. Last week he'd taken the big truck with a load up to Franklin, WV for the Treasure Mountain Festival. Sometime later this week, he'd run a load to Kingwood, WV for the Buckwheat Festival and another to Springs, Pa. for the Folk Festival in the small town of 300. Also, the

Jay Heavner

Autumn Glory Festival people in Oakland, Md. wanted a small amount, only half a truckload, to test out this year. They'd heard of his product from others in the area and wanted to see how well it sold before giving him all their business. He was fine with that. They would be back for more, he was sure. Right now, he had all the business he could handle.

Tom entered the building and quickly found the orders for the Cumberland run. His truck would be full this morning, and he loaded it carefully with the fork truck. Just the other day, one of the drivers turned too swiftly, and a full pallet fell to the concrete floor. Fortunately, no one was hurt, but they had a driver's meeting shortly afterward on the safe operation of a forklift. With water, the mess to clean up was minimal, unlike soft drinks or beer, but someone could have been seriously hurt or worse, and there was also the dollar loss from damaged product and clean up.

He opened the large door and drove the truck out of the warehouse. At this hour, he would be just ahead of the early morning traffic. Who would have ever thought that WV Route 28 would ever have a rush hour? But with the delivery trucks, school buses, people going to work and normal through traffic, it was quite hectic in the morning and again in the afternoon. Finding an opening, he rolled the truck out onto the highway. A mile later, he passed the Old Furnace Restaurant, and the parking lot was full. *Bet they're as busy as a one-armed paper hanger.* Before long, he made the left turn onto Alternate WV Route 28 that took him to Ridgeley, WV, and on to Cumberland, Md. The old road down the side of the mountain was narrow with no shoulder for pull-offs and not one of Tom's favorite highways. He slowed to 25 mph as he reached the town of Ridgeley. The old high school where he narrowly escaped arrest some years before was still there but was now a middle school. Oh, how he wished to relive and changed the events that happened, but he realized if he could, he would not be the man he was today. *Funny how things work out*, he thought.

Tom rolled the truck through the small town. His truck barely fit under the Western Maryland Railroad viaduct. He noted the damage done to the underpass by those who missed the warning signs. Not too long ago, a semi unsuccessfully attempted to pass through the low passage and what a mess that made. Traffic was tied up for nearly half a day as workers removed the stuck and damaged eighteen-wheeler.

He made a tight S turn, went past the state historical marker telling about Fort Ohio, the old blockhouse the Ohio Company built in the 1700s when this area was the American frontier. Soon he crossed the Blue bridge over the Potomac River into Maryland and stopped for the light at the intersection with Green Street. Traffic from I 68 rumbled overhead on the cross-town elevated highway. To his right sat the old, small, log building that served as Colonel George Washington's headquarters while he served with English General Edward Braddock during the French and Indian War in the mid-1700s. *It's a shame*, thought Tom, how little the local people know about the rich history of their area.

The light changed to green, and Tom swung the truck left onto Greene Street, and his first stop was the Sheetz convenience store a few blocks away. He made another left into the parking lot and pulled into the delivery area. Sheetz would be getting their normal quantity. They'd been an excellent addition to his clientele when they moved into the area. A figure on the little rise next to the store caught his eye. It was Carole, better known as Crazy Carole, by the people of Cumberland. She was a homeless person with schizophrenia, and Tom knew her. Two plastic bags at her feet contained everything she owned, and she wore a tan sleeveless top and shorts that came to mid-thigh. Her arms were around her body, and she stood shivering in the cold morning air. Tom had a special place in his heart for the people like her as he knew first-hand about mental illness. His older son, Brian, had schizophrenia and took his own life to escape the madness.

Tom reached behind the seat and searched through a bag of assorted clothes; all his drivers carried for times such as these. Joann, his wife, picked them up at thrift stores around the area. He found a jacket and some blue jeans that should fit Carole. Carefully, he folded them, got out of the truck, and walked across the concrete parking lot toward the shivering woman.

"Carole," he called. "Carole, it's Tom."

She turned her head toward him, and a bit of a smile came to her face. "Hi, Tom," she said without emotion. This was not their first meeting. Whenever Tom was able, he would stop from his duties, talk with her, and usually give her a $10 bill to help her that day.

"I've got something here to help keep you warm."

She looked into the bag Tom gave her and said to him, "Thank you." Her small smile grew a bit. She took the jacket out of the bag and quickly put it on. Next, she stepped into the blue jeans, pulled them up over her bare legs, and buttoned them at the waist. She pulled the zipper up, looked at Tom, and again said, "Thank you," and nothing more.

"Are you hungry?" asked Tom. She nodded her head, yes. "Well, how about I get you and me a couple of egg and bacon biscuits, some tater tots and coffee over there?" And he pointed to Sheetz. She nodded her head again, and they walked down the hill to the store with Carole carrying her two ragged sacks of possessions. Tom opened the door and directed Carole to a small booth that could accommodate four people with two on each side. "Sit here, and I'll get us the food."

"Okay," she said, sat down, and placed her bags on the chair next to her.

Tom walked to the fast food section of the convenience store, ordered and quickly received their breakfast items in a paper bag. He walked over to where Carole was sitting, placed the bag on the table between them, and sat down directly across from her. The warm food smelled mouthwatering, and Carole's little smile grew slightly bigger. He took the food out of the bag and placed the items before them. She quickly grabbed the big biscuit and began eating hungrily. Tom bowed his head and blessed the food. Carole noted her *faux pas* and quit eating. Tom mouthed an amen and opened his eyes, which met Carole's. "Did you bless it for me too, Tom?" she asked. He nodded his head yes, and she said, "Thank you," again.

"So how are you, Carole? What's new with you? I see you're not at the treatment center. Are you taking your meds?"

"Oh, I'm okay, more or less." Again she smiled a little, took another bite of her meal, and sipped on the hot coffee.

"You know you would do better if you took your medicine and the treatment they give at the center."

"Don't wanna go back there while she is there! She is evil! Don't wanna go back there unless she is gone."

"Who is she, and why don't you like her?"

"Noela Chateaux. She molested me while I was there once. I'll scratch her eyes out if I ever get the chance. She's got it coming. I've been in a couple of times since, but never got the chance. They keep her away from me now, and the last time I was there, she was on vacation. I'll hurt her bad. All I need is the opportunity. She's got it coming."

Tom was taken back. "Didn't you tell anyone? Didn't they do something?"

Carole looked at Tom like he was stupid. "They didn't do nothin'. Nobody believed me. After all, I'm Crazy Carole. Nobody believes me."

"I'm sorry. That's terrible. Wish there was something I could do."

"Don't worry about it. My lawyer friend gets me out now when they haul me in. We got an agreement."

Tom was puzzled. "An agreement?"

"Yeah, he gets me out of the happy hotel, and I sleep with him. A girl's got to do what a girl got to do. Sometimes I turn tricks here around town too for money to live." Carole sipped at the coffee and took a bite of the potato patty, part of the combo meal deal.

"Tom," said Carole, "I could make you feel real good in your big truck when we're done here."

"I don't think so, Carole. My wife takes care of all those needs, and I'm not looking for anything more, okay?"

She was quiet for a moment and said, "Good. I'm glad you said that. I thought I could trust you, and now I'm sure." Tom let out a sigh of relief, but he wasn't sure where this conversation was going. She spoke again, "I didn't know how you'll take this, but the Death Angel is sitting in the chair next to you."

Tom was surprised, to say the least, but he was with Crazy Carole. "The Death Angel? What's he look like?"

"Well, he's dressed in a black suit and pretty ordinary. I doubt you'd even notice him if you passed him on the street. You wanna know something else?"

"Sure, why not."

"He says a breath of wind came out of nowhere and turned the bullet meant to kill you at the farm at Patterson Creek." Tom looked at her suspiciously. *Was she making this up? She could have deduced some of the details from the article in the Cumberland Times-News and be making up the rest.* "He says the big Indian took the bullet meant for you in Vietnam."

Tom's jaw dropped, and his eyes widened. *How could she know? He knew he'd never told her anything about the battle at Ia Drang. There was no way she could know unless...* "What else does he say?"

"He says he was there. It was his job to make sure you were out of the way, and so far, he's failed, but he's waiting for the right time now."

A cold chill went down Tom's back, and the hairs on his arms stood up. "Does he have anything else to say?"

"He says he doesn't understand humans. The same hand that caresses and serves can be a fist for hurting. He doesn't understand why people are like they are, and he would really like a vacation, too. The dying is getting him down, but he has a job to do. Oh, he just left, but before he did, he said, 'Noela Chateaux and just desserts.'"

"Carole, you're freakin' me out with this. And what did he mean by Noela Chateaux and just desserts?"

"I don't know. Sometimes he's pretty straight forward. Sometimes he's very cryptic. I don't know." They sat in silence and finished their meals.

When they were done, Tom got up and spoke, "Well, me lady," he said in his best Cockney accent, "We's best to be a-goin'. The King needs our labors and taxes."

She offered him her hand, he took it, and she rose from her seat. "Yes, we's best to be off. For King and County," she said in her best Cockney, too.

Tom nodded to her, and they headed to the front of the store, and out the door they went. A man who looked homeless stood at the front of the store. A cigarette drooped from his lips, and he held a Styrofoam cup in his hand. Tom reached into his pocket for spare change and dropped it in the cup. "Hey, the man growled angrily. That was my morning coffee!"

"Oh, sorry," apologized Tom. He reached into his wallet and pulled out a $10 bill he gave to the grubby man.

The man smiled and said, "Mister, you can do that again, anytime. I like the money. Better yet, just give me a $10 when you wanna drop your change in my coffee again."

Tom smiled. "Sure, I'll remember that next time." Tom and Carole walked over to his truck. He gave her a $20 bill and climbed into his vehicle. "You be careful, Carole."

"Will do, and thanks," she replied. "I think you need to be more careful than me." She had a somber look on her face.

"I will," Tom replied. He gave the truck some gas, crossed the parking lot, and pulled onto Greene Street. He looked into the rearview mirror and saw Carole waving goodbye. "You be careful," he mouthed to himself. "And I think I'd better do that, too."

***

On the other side of Cumberland just east of the Crosstown Bridge, Officer Todd Bowman threaded his way down the shoulder of Interstate 68 to the wreck. He'd been enjoying his morning coffee and an egg with bacon biscuit at Mason's Barn Restaurant a mile away when he got the call. No donuts for him. Traffic had backed up due to construction work on the crosstown bridge. *Wasn't that thing always under repair?* And someone plowed into the back of a stopped big rig. He pulled the patrol car up behind the other Maryland State Police Crown Victoria patrol car and exited. Another officer was looking at the carnage. Todd recognized him as the new guy, Matt Mynheir, who had just transferred in from the Baltimore

Division. Todd walked up to the other cop. "What have we got here, Matt?"

"Not pretty, Todd. Some woman drove her car under the back of the eighteen-wheeler. Stuff's everywhere, including her head in the back seat. Sheared it right off. Not too damaged though, the head that is. I've seen a lot worse."

The two troopers searched for information in the vehicle as to the identity of the dead woman. Todd found a clamshell cell phone open and still active. "Looks like she was texting when she hit the truck and eating a burger, too." He looked at the severed head. "And smoking a cigarette. Some people must have a death wish."

"Did you find a wallet or a purse with some ID?" questioned Trooper Mynheir, as he attempted to open the trunk. "Got it," he said as it opened. "Let's see if I can find anything of interest in here."

"Hey, I found her purse," said Trooper Bowman, "And it's got a wallet in it. Let's see. The driver's license of the dearly departed says 'Noela Chateaux.' And I found another ID. It seems she worked for a mental unit here in the city."

"Noela Chateaux. I can't believe it. When I worked in Baltimore, we had been trying for years to get her on charges for molesting children. The warrant for her arrest just came in a little while ago. We got the right one. Her trunk is full of kiddy porn, lots of older women with children doing all kinds of sick things."

Trooper Bowman walked back to the trunk and looked in. "Now, that is disgusting." They closed the trunk, walked to the impact area, and surveyed the mess. Todd noted the truck was from McDonalds. The mural on the side of the truck had the classic golden arches and said, "New at McDonalds, Get your Just Desserts now, Strawberry and Cherry Flavors."

"Now, this is funny," said Trooper Bowman.

"What's so funny about a headless dead woman?" asked the second trooper.

"Look at the truck."

The second trooper did and chucked. "Now, I see. Looks like she got her just desserts alrighty."

"If you aren't a sick puppy when you get this job, you will be shortly," and with that comment, they both laughed. "Gonna be a long day clearing this mess up." With that, the other man got his camera out of his patrol car and started taking pictures needed for the investigation of the accident. *Yup, gonna be a long day.*

Jay Heavner

Chapter 16

Tom was up early Monday morning, really early. It was not one of those nights where his PTSD caused him to toss and turn the whole time. No, he'd had a good, restful sleep. Sunday was a good day, and he taught at his little church on the Beatitudes. How well he remembered the actual site from his ten-day trip to the Holy Land sometime before. Sunday lunch was a feast fit for a king, made by Joann. A short nap, which he liked to call a "snap," rounded out the afternoon. It was early evening when he received a phone call changing his plans for Monday. Doug, his son and manager of the bottled water business Tom started, called him. Buddy, one of their drivers and employees, called in with good and bad news. The good news, he was the proud father of a 7 pound 3-ounce baby boy. The bad news, they took the newborn back to the hospital because of jaundice. On the way home, he'd been rear-ended, and the car was totaled. He seemed to be unhurt, but he wanted to be checked thoroughly by a doctor, so he was taking a sick day. Doug shifted the deliveries with the men he knew would be coming in, but he was still short, and that's where Tom came in. Doug had another call, one from White Tails Resort. Their two-day music festival had been a roaring success because of the great weather over the weekend. Attendance had far exceeded their expectations. They used all the extra bottled water Tom's company supplied for the event and most of the remaining bottled water that was on site. They needed to be refilled ASAP.

Tom ate a bowl of muesli and downed two cups of coffee, Chock Full o' Nuts of course, to kick-start the morning. By 6:30, he had the big flat-bed loaded completely full with pallets of water. All he needed now was the paperwork, and he would be off. His cell phone in his pocket began to ring. He took it out and looked at the number on the caller ID. Why, it was his old friend Padre, the Father of the local Catholic Church. *Wonder what he wanted?*

"Hello, Padre, long time no see. What's up with you on your day off?" asked Tom.

"Thought we might have breakfast and talk. You up for that?"

"Sure am. I've got a water run, and I'm heading for Cumberland. Can you meet me somewhere there?"

"Sure can. How 'bout that new place in the south end, Rock of Ages Restaurant, I think it's called."

"I know where it is, on Virginia Avenue across from the railroad roundhouse. I've not been in there, but have been told it's good and reasonably priced."

"That's the place. I have something I need to talk with you about."

"Thought that might be the case. My fee for pastoral consultation is breakfast, deal?"

"Tom, you drive a hard bargain, but you work cheap. It's a deal. I'll be leaving the church in a minute, so I'll be a little behind you, okay?"

"Okay, I'll find us a good table out of the way so we can talk without too many prying ears."

"Sounds like a plan, Tom. See you soon."

Tom hung up the phone. *Wonder what he needs to talk about? It must be important if he gave in to buying breakfast so quickly. Guess I'll find out soon.*

The paperwork for the bill went quickly, and Tom was on the road to Cumberland in no time. He noted some tire skid marks at an S turn and saw some broken glass, pieces of plastic, and a dark stain in the road. *Looks like we had another wreck on Bloody Route 28. When is the state ever going to do something to fix this highway?*

A short while later, he crossed the bridge over the Potomac River into Cumberland, Maryland. The old towpath of the C & O Canal paralleled the river from its end in Cumberland to its beginning near Washington, D.C. Old George had sure played a big part in the development of the area, including the canal. *I wonder what life was like back in Washington's day and later when the canal was operating?*

He turned onto River Street and three blocks later, pulled to a stop at the intersection with Virginia Avenue. At that odd, five-way intersection, he made a quick left and shortly afterward pulled into the parking lot at the Rock of Ages Restaurant. After finding a spot where he was confident the big truck would not get blocked in, he walked across Bowen Street and up to the door. The large sign on the glass read, "Rock of Ages Restaurant and Christian Night Club." A painting of Christ on the cross covered the remainder of the door. He went in and asked for a booth in a corner. The waitress named Sandy showed him one out of the way and gave him a menu. Tom said he was expecting a friend and needed a few minutes, which she gave him. The menu contained the usual breakfasts he expected. Sandy returned and asked what drinks and meals they wanted. Tom ordered two house breakfast specials: two scrambled eggs, two bacon strips, grits, a biscuit, and coffee. The coffee arrived quickly, steaming hot. About five minutes later, Padre arrived dressed in regular street clothes and sat down. "Never been here. Looks like your standard good eatin' place. How's Tom doin' today?" he inquired.

Tom said he was doing alright, and he had taken the liberty of ordering for both of them. Padre said that was fine. He was in a hurry, too. The food came quickly, and after a short blessing by the Padre, it proved not only to look tasty but was very tasty. The men ate like hungry bears. Tom took a big drink of coffee to wash down the last of the scrambled eggs. "Now, what was it you needed to talk with me about?" he asked.

Father Frank looked up and paused. He said nothing for what seemed a full minute but was only a few seconds. He looked around to see if anyone was near. The other patrons were on the far side of the restaurant and busy in their own conversations. He sipped the coffee and swallowed hard. "I ah, I ah, don't really know where to begin. I have a confession to make."

"Whoa! Stop right there. You know I don't do confessions. That's something you guys do. If you need to confess something, you need to see a priest, *comprende*?"

Father Frank grimaced. "Tom, please hear me out, and you'll understand."

"Okay, but you are kinda weirding me out on this confession thing."

The Padre ignored the last remark and continued. "I hardly know where to start. I feel like such a hypocrite."

"Okay." The Padre had Tom's full attention. "Let's start at the beginning."

"Yesterday, after church, my secretary, Janice Rae, asked to see me in private. It seemed really awkward the way she asked. She was not her usual friendly, cordial self. Something was wrong. There was tension in her voice and manner. Some people stayed late and asked a lot of good questions about my sermon and the Christian faith. After about ten minutes, they left, and I was able to talk with her. I asked her what was wrong, and she laid into me with accusations of being seen with a woman last week holding her hand and kissing her passionately on the lips. 'What I fraud I was,' she said, 'I wasn't a committed Christian fit for the Priesthood. It's nothing but a facade. I wasn't who I said I was.' As you can imagine, I was taken back and shocked. She went to say she saw me and the woman at the Frederick Square Mall in Frederick, Maryland."

Tom's eyes were wide open. "And what happened then?"

"Tom, I hadn't been to Frederick in months. When I got over the initial shock of what she said, I realized she saw my twin brother and his wife, who live in Frederick."

"So, what did you do?"

"Well, as delicately as I could, I explained the situation to her. When she grasped the veracity of my statement, she was visibly shaken, embarrassed, and devastated, yet relieved all at the same time. She was a mess. I consoled her and explained I could understand her mistake as we are identical. She was still shaken, so I reassured her that as a Christian and a priest, I was glad she held me accountable. Only a true friend who cared would risk ending their friendship and professional relationship. It still took a moment or so for her to gain her composure, but she was satisfied with the answer. Being a twin has got me in a lot of trouble at times."

"How so?"

"My brother Fred and I went from a junior high school of 300 students to a high school with 3000. We were big for our ages, but still, things happened. The first week we were there, these four big guys came up to us and said, 'We beat the crap outta twins,' only they didn't say crap. My brother's always been a fast thinker, and he told them we were triplets, not twins. Anyone who messed with one, messes with all three of us. They wanted to know where the third was, so he said he'd get him. He went to his locker, changed his shirt and jacket, messed up his hair, and came back. Said he was Fallon and anyone who messes with one of us messes with all three of us. They backed off and never gave us any more trouble, although a lot of twins suffered from those four in high school. At graduation, they came over to us and asked where Fallon was. We told them he was flunking Mr. Miller's math class. He dropped out and would be taking a summer class so he could graduate. That satisfied them, and they were never the wiser."

"I have to say that's a remarkable story, but why do I have the feeling there's more to this story. Level with me, Padre. What's up?"

He dropped his eyes to the table and then looked Tom square in the eye. The Padre began, "I met a gal named Stacy, a woman about my age when I was at one of the district meetings in Pittsburgh. She was a counselor at a Catholic school in Aliquippa. We enjoyed each other's company, and I made it a point not to miss monthly district meetings as did she. She gave me her phone number. One thing led to another. I've been seeing her every Monday on our days off for some time. Tom, we fell in love. Can you believe it? Me? A priest? I know it's crazy, but it happened. Now, do you see? I feel like such a fool."

There was a long pause before Tom said, "I really don't know what to say. I never saw this coming."

"Neither did I. Neither did I," he repeated. "And there's more. She told me a month ago she was pregnant, and I know it's my child. I'm so torn up inside. And I love her. Can you believe this? Me, a priest at that?"

"So, what are you gonna do?" Tom asked.

"The right thing. Today, after I leave here, I'm driving to Pittsburgh, and we're having a clerk of the county court marry us. Next Sunday, I'll be resigning from my position at my church. After that, I'll be moving in with her. I have a few ideas for work. We'll see what happens. Tom, I was born a thousand years too late. Priests back then could get married and have families, but some old Pope had a revelation, so he said, and we can't do it today. Now, do you see why I wanted to talk, but was afraid of what you would say?"

Tom looked at the big black man across the booth from him. His eyes begged for acceptance and looked like they were tearing up. Tom said, "Padre, you've always been my friend, and I will support you in any way I can. Do what you think and know is right. And above all know this, not one word you've told me here today will I spill. This was in strict confidence as a pastor and friend. I love you, my Christian brother, and want nothing but the best for you and Stacy. Can we pray?" Padre nodded yes. He reached his two large hands out across the table to Tom. Tom clutched the powerful hands, lowered his head as did the Padre. He began, "Almighty God, You know all. You know us inside and out. You know what is in a man's heart. I'm here with my brother in Christ today. He's hurting, and he's one of Yours. Direct his path as only You can do in the way that is right. Comfort his heart and bless him in this. We ask in Jesus' name. Amen."

"And a second amen to that," Father Frank said as tears ran down his cheeks. "A big, second amen."

The two men rose from their seats and embraced in a bear hug.

"I'll never forget this, Tom. Thank you. You're a true brother."

"You're my brother, too." He paused and said, "Hey, we have things to do. You gonna pay for this so we can go?"

"Yeah, guess it's on me." Father Frank caught the eye of Sandy the waitress. He asked, "Will a $20 cover this?"

"Yes, it will," she said.

"Keep everything left for your tip."

"Thanks," she replied. "You guys be sure and come again."

"We'll be back. Take care, and God bless," Tom added.

Sandy joyfully said, "He really does. His mercies are new every morning. Great is His faithfulness."

"Amen to that," the deep voice of the Padre said.

The two men walked to the back and left the building. They stopped next to the Padre's car. Tom looked at his big friend and spoke, "I don't know what more to say, brother. Just want you to know when you need me, I'll be there."

"I know, brother, I know." The big man spread his arms, and the two men hugged again like true agape friends. Tears poured down the big man's face. "I know. I know you'll be there."

The two men parted, and the Padre got in his car. Tom stood nearby as Father Frank wiped the tears from his eyes, sniffled and said, "Well, just like Smokey and the Bandit, I have a long way to go and a short time to get there. I'll see you later and hope and pray this all works out. Later."

"Yeah, see you later." The car backed out into the street, went the short distance to Virginia Avenue, and disappeared in the railroad viaduct.

Never saw that coming, thought Tom. *Wonder what other surprises are waiting for me today?*

Chapter 17

Tom drove the truck through the twisting, narrow streets of Cumberland. He stopped at a supermarket and numerous convenience stores before backing into the loading dock at the *Cumberland Times-News* in downtown Cumberland, Maryland. Here he had been kidnapped place and threatened with death if he did not tell his captors where the lost gold payroll of General Braddock was buried. A dreadful feeling went through Tom as he thought of this and he tried to push those thoughts to the deep recesses of his mind but had little success. The order today was mainly five-gallon bottles for the coolers, plus a few cases of the small six-ounce mini bottles. Tom fixed the long, multi-use hand truck in the heavy-duty position with all four wheels on the floor. One large and heavy load should do it. How often Tom wished he was in the chip and snack-food business. Not the physically demanding bottled-water business, but he wasn't. He buzzed the secured door to gain entrance. The door clicked; he opened the service door and pushed the loaded cart up the hallway to the elevator. Here, he'd been knocked unconscious and kidnapped earlier in the year. He hit the elevator button and waited. The lift doors parted, and he pushed the cart into the lift. He touched the number two button and felt the box rise. A bell alerted him as the box stopped, the doors opened, he made his way through the building and dropped the cargo off in the utility closet. Tom heard a muffled voice behind him, jumped around, and came face to face with the owner of the newspaper, Mr. Godfrey. "Oh, so sorry to startle you, Mr. Kenney. I should have known better after what happened to you here. I am so sorry."

Jay Heavner

Tom felt his heart in his throat, and it beat heavily against his chest. "You liked to scare the crap outta me!"

"I am so sorry. Please, finish up what you are doing and bring the bill to my office. I want to pay up my account with your company."

Tom took the last of the five-gallon bottles from the cart and placed them on a heavy-duty metal rack bolted to a block wall. He folded the wheels up, which made the utility cart into a more standard and moveable two-wheeled hand truck. Mr. Godfrey was waiting, and Tom followed him to his office. The walls were filled with plaques and framed pictures about the paper and its owner.

"Please, have a seat," said Mr. Godfrey. He pulled out a legal-size checkbook, looked at another book, saw what he wanted, and began to write a check. "Oh, I almost forgot. I need today's bill to bring this totally up to date."

Tom handed him the bill of sale and looked around the room at the memorabilia. He could see Mr. Godfrey must own at least ten newspapers, maybe more and noted many pictures of him with various dignitaries from the local and state level all the way to the national level. Tom recognized several past and present members of Congress and one past President. He knew Mr. Godfrey had money and connections, but this surprised Tom. Here was a man of quiet power.

Mr. Godfrey finished writing the check and handed it to Tom. He'd seen Tom looking at the items on the walls. "What do you think, Mr. Kenney? What do you think of all this?"

"I'm somewhat surprised. You seem like such a down to earth kind of guy. I would have never known."

"With great power comes great responsibility. I have seen it go to the head of many people, male and female. I have tried never to forget where I came from and let it go to my head. For many people, vast power created deep, deep troubles that swallowed them. A fire can warm or consume you."

Tom noted an article from the local paper framed on the wall about General Braddock and his lost payroll and asked Mr. Godfrey what he knew on the subject.

"Oh, just what I read in the newspaper," he chuckled. "I keep it there to remind me to not become overconfident like the British General. He should have listened to George Washington and not made the Indian scouts and warriors mad enough to leave. But he was somewhat of a pompous man, and it cost him dearly. One should listen to those around him for their advice."

Tom agreed. The two men made some small talk about the economic state of western Maryland. Both agreed it was not right, and the people on the coast and Annapolis cared little about what happened west of Frederick. The local joke was the state of Maryland wanted to sell its three western counties to West Virginia or Pennsylvania as a means of balancing the budget their spendthrift Governor and Legislature recently passed.

"Oh, I must be keeping you from your work, Mr. Kenney. Let me walk with you to the loading dock and see to your safety." Tom grimaced. They walked through the building, took the elevator down, and went through the hallway where Tom had been attacked. Mr. Godfrey opened the service door. They exited the building onto the outdoor loading dock. A loud truck horn's blasting caught their attention. Someone had pulled in front of a newly painted Yuengling's beer truck advertising "Braddock's Gold, Our New Premium Lager. We guarantee you'll love it."

Both men looked at the commotion in the nearby street. The driver in the car yelled an obscenity at the truck driver even though he was at fault and could have been killed if not for the quick action of the truck driver.

Tom looked at Mr. Godfrey. "Just makes you wonder about some people."

"Yes, it does. He nearly found Braddock's gold today." And he chuckled.

Tom chuckled, too. "You don't know much about Braddock's gold?"

Mr. Godfrey chuckled again. "Only what I read in my newspaper." He paused, "and on the side of beer trucks." He smiled.

Tom smiled, too. "Guess I'd better be going. Thank you for the check and your personal insight. I'll remember it. Got to get crackin'. Places to go and water to deliver. Thanks again."

"My pleasure. I hope I said something insightful and useful. I hope to talk to you soon. Have a great day."

"A mega ditto on that," said Tom as he climbed into his truck. He pulled onto the street and passed the beer truck parked in front of a local watering hole. *Braddock's Gold.* Mr. Godfrey had given him something to think about.

Chapter 18

It was early morning when the telephone woke Tom. The sun peeked in his bedroom window, facing the east. He looked at his caller ID and saw the number from the Catholic Church in Fort Ashby. "Hello," he said, wiping the sleepers from his eyes. "This Padre?"

"Yes, it's me. Hate to wake you, but I need your help." Tom thought that might be the case. A week had passed since Father Frank went to Pittsburgh, and he needed an update. "Two things, I want to talk with you over breakfast, brunch, or lunch, whatever we can work out. And then I have some horrible news. The building at the square in Fort Ashby, where Cindy's Restaurant is located, burned down last night, and they can't find three people. One of the volunteer firemen called me early. They don't think they got out. I think we need to be there to provide any comfort we can for family and the first responders."

Tom was now wide awake and sitting up in bed. "Wow, I think you are right. It's not going to be a pleasant scene. I'll get over there as soon as I can. Anything else?"

"Not for now. I'll save the rest of the news, most of it bad, till we eat. See you soon. Bye."

"Bye."

Tom sat on the bed in disbelief. It seemed the big, old building had stood there forever—now it was gone. Suddenly, it hit him—three members of his little church, the Dowlen family, lived in one of the apartments on the second floor. He hated to hear of untimely deaths of anyone, and he so hoped it wasn't those people he came to know and love. They left the Middle East because of religious persecution and somehow found their way to Fort Ashby, West Virginia. Eli, the father aged thirty, still carried a large scar on his forehead from a knife attack by a mob of fanatics who tried to kill him. He and his wife, Hannah, both spoke broken English, which was sometimes hard to understand, but their daughter, Ruhama, spoke English as good as Arabic. Joann rolled over and looked at him with half-awake eyes. "Mmmm," she said, "who was it?"

"Padre with bad news. The old block building behind the Custard Stand in Fort Ashby burned down last night, and they can't locate three people. He asked me to come with him and help anyone who may need our kind of assistance."

Joann woke with a start. "What? That's terrible." She rubbed her eyes and asked, "How soon will you be leaving?"

'Within the next five minutes. I remembered for once to set the coffee on autopilot. It should be ready, and I'll grab a fruit bar, an apple, and of course, a bottle of water."

"Tom, why don't you grab a couple of cases? Bet there's some thirsty people over there this morning."

"Good idea, I'll do that."

The couple dressed quickly, and Tom went to the warehouse for two cases of water. He placed them in a small wagon and pulled it to his old Chevy truck. The water was sitting on the floor where the passenger's feet would normally be. He walked back into the house, and Joann had his coffee ready in a big cup with a lid. At one time, Tom liked to place the hot, lidless drink between his legs for easy access, but a sudden stop with spilled liquids on his various body parts made him see the wisdom to a cup with a good lid. It only took one time. As the saying goes, 'if you want to be stupid, you got to be tough,' and Tom did not like to do stupid more than once. She gave him a small paper bag containing two apples and several fruit bars and said, "I'll tell Doug what happened. I hope he can get along without you today."

"He should be able to. I was planning on doing about a half-day on paperwork and then goin' fishin'. Give me a call if he's in a pinch and has to have me, okay?"

"Aye, aye, Captain. Can I pray before you go?"

"Yes, I think this situation will call for a lot of prayer. Please start."

"Precious Lord, we don't always know why things happen in this fallen world, but we do know you will never leave us, and we can find comfort in that. Be with my husband, Padre, the firemen, and all who are at the square ministering help each in their ownway. Thank You for Your Son Jesus You sent to redeem us and save us from sin. Amen."

"Amen. Got to go. Call me if they can't get by without me here."

"Will do and Tom?" she paused. "I love you."

"Love you too, honey. See you sometime this afternoon, I suspect. Bye."

Joann said, "Bye," and Tom was off down the highway.

As Tom drove the ten miles to Fort Ashby, he had time to think and pray. He needed all the strength available as he feared the worst. Rounding an S turn, he passed a metal building under construction. Rumor had it his area was getting its first Dollar Store. As he went by the gap in Knobley Mountain, which WV Route 956 ran through, he saw the fog still hanging in the Potomac River Valley though it had lifted where he was. A yellow Mineral County school bus waited to turn out onto WV 28, the road Tom was traveling. Fortunately for him, he got by before it, or he would have had to follow the bus all the way to Fort Ashby. There was no place to pass on the crooked mountain road, nor any place for the bus to pull over. Something needed to be done about this road, but it seemed the state just did not care. He rode past the old two-story gas station with the huge American flag painted on the front. Maybe someday it would reopen, but he was not holding his breath. Onward, he continued over the short concrete bridge that spanned Turners Run. The stream never ran dry even in the worst droughts because of the gushing springs at its headwaters in the gap.

The Catholic Church where Padre was Priest passed by on his left. Father Frank's car was already gone, and as usual, the Padre had something thought-provoking on the church marquee. "Choose life," it said. "Your mother did." *Amen to that. How many people his age with kids and grandkids would have been killed in the womb if abortion was legal years ago when they were conceived?*

He rode on down to Siple's curve and found lots of skid marks on the road. It looked like another bad accident occurred recently. The wind was blowing from Freddie's big barn, and Tom got a good whiff of cows. *Nothing like the pungent smell of ripe manure to greet you in the morning.* The road to the town of Patterson Creek paralleled the stream with the same name intersected WV 28 on the left. One mile later, he drove over the William Shuck Memorial Bridge spanning Patterson Creek. Tom was almost there and dreaded what he would find. He passed several gas stations, the Fort Ashby Bookstore, and The Talk of the Town Restaurant. The light was green, but he had to wait for a State Trooper directing traffic at the town square. Tom looked to where the large two-story block building should be, but all he could see were smoke and some flames coming from the chaotic ruins. Traffic moved, but the State Trooper blocked Tom as he attempted to pull into the parking lot. "No stopping," he growled. "Keep moving."

Tom looked at the man in blue and said, "I'm Pastor Tom Kenney. They called and asked me to come help."

The cop's demeanor changed. He walked over to the red danger tape surrounding the scene and lifted it up. "This way," he said and shook his head. "It ain't pretty."

Tom found a tight spot to park among the many vehicles at the scene. The whole building was gone. Emergency vehicles from Fort Ashby, Short Gap, Patterson Creek, Springfield, Fountain, and Keyser sat nearby. Tom could not remember seeing this many fire trucks together in Fort Ashby except at the annual Mineral County Fair Parade. Smoke from the fire irritated his nose, and he sensed something else he had not smelled since the battle decades before in the Ia Drang Valley in Vietnam, the smell of burned flesh. Someone died here. For a moment, he thought he saw two Huey helicopters carrying off the dead and wounded. He closed his eyes. *No, I'm not in Vietnam. I'm in Fort Ashby, West Virginia, and people needed me.* Tom opened his eyes, and the sight of a burned-out building returned to his eyes. He hoped this was just a hallucination, too, but no, this was real. He got out of the truck and grabbed his ball cap that said CCFA for Calvary Chapel Fort Ashby. Among the firemen in their yellow protective suits and hats, he saw Father Frank. He said hello to several of them who returned the greeting. Hoping for a good report, but fearing the worst, he asked the Padre, "How are things. It looks bad."

Father Frank nodded, "It is. The building is a total loss, and the firemen still can't account for three people. They think they've located some bodies near where they believe the fire started." He pointed to an area the firemen were hosing down heavily. Tom's stomach churned involuntarily. The place he pointed at was directly below where the Dowlen's apartment had been.

One of the firemen shouted," I found something." Two other men hosed the area down as they moved closer. "Yeah, I found one of them."

More men carrying a stretcher moved into the location. The first group shoved some more debris out of the way, looked down, and stopped. They waved for the stretcher-bearers to come. Gently the men picked up the charred human remains, put them on the stretcher, and covered them with a tarp of some sort. They carefully walked out of the debris field while carrying the burden laden stretcher. They walked behind a screen the coroner had erected. "Hey," came a shout from the fireman who had made the first gruesome discover, "I found two more."

Carefully, stretcher-bearers went twice more into the ruins, retrieved the bodies, and took them behind the screen. Tom walked over, but a Deputy from Hampshire County stopped him. "You can't go over there. Official business only."

"I'm Pastor Tom Kenney. I think I can identify the bodies."

The deputy was not yielding an inch. "Official business only," he repeated firmly.

"He's okay." Tom and the Hampshire County Deputy turned toward the voice. "I know him. Let him pass," said Mineral County Sheriff Wagoner.

The Deputy moved to the side, and Tom walked behind the curtain. The coroner had watched the tense conversation and motioned for him to come closer. "You think you can identify the bodies? They're pretty burned."

"I think I know who they are," Tom said. A lump which felt the size of a grapefruit was in his throat and he feared the worst. The coroner pulled back the tarp on the first body and looked at Tom. He nodded, and the coroner covered it. They proceeded to the second body and did the same. Tom nodded again, and the coroner continued his grim work with the third. Tom nodded again and the coroner returned the covering to the body. Tom said, "The first body is Mr. Dowlen. The second is his wife, and I think the third has to be their daughter. It's hard to tell. The body was so badly burned."

The coroner nodded. "Thank you for your help. We'll get dental records for a positive ID, but we know where to start. Are you okay? You look like you've seen a ghost. This isn't easy business."

Tom was not alright. The charred bodies reminded him of the North Vietnam Regulars burned by napalm dropped in the war. A few Americans also died from the firebombs in the three-day battle. They were about to be overrun, and the close air raids were the only way to save any of the US forces. Unfortunately, a few of the bombs were off target and hit friendlies. He could still hear the screams of men he knew as the flaming jell burned them to death. "I'll be okay," he said as he walked away.

A big arm grabbed him as he stumbled. "Whoa, Tom. You're not looking so good. Let me get you a place to sit down for a spell." His friend the Padre had found him and took him to a folding chair someone had left for the first responders.

"I'll be okay. Just give me a moment," Tom said.

Padre looked at him sideways. "Tom, I haven't seen that shade of green since watching Kermit the Frog on the *Muppet Show*. You sit there and take all the time you need. You'll be alright, and there are others here that need my help."

"Okay, whatever you say." Father Frank studied him some more. "Really, I'll be okay," said Tom as he tried to smile.

"Give yourself a break, Tom. I'll be nearby if you need me. Just holler." Father Frank smiled at Tom and then left. Tom watched as he went to a crying couple. He talked to them, and soon those big black comforting arms engulfed the two. Tom thought he saw a tear run from the Padre's eye. His genuine love and compassion for people hurting was the biggest reason so many of the town's folks opened their hearts to him.

Tom sat for a few moments, regaining his composure. The scene reminded him of the organized confusion of battle; only today's fight was with an enemy as deadly as any human foe, fire. He felt an arm on his shoulder. Surprised, he turned to see Mr. Godfrey and a woman next to him.

Tom said, "Mr. Godfrey, you snuck up on me. You seem to be everywhere. Guess the fire got your attention. You two here covering it for the Cumberland paper?"

"Yes, it is the big story in the Tri-state area today. I was at the office today when I heard the calls coming in over the police band. Oh, where are my manners? This is Joyce Lynn. She's one of our new reporters at the paper. She does photography, too."

"Pleased to meet you, Miss Joyce Lynn."

She replied, "It's actually Mrs. Joyce Lynn, but I would prefer you call me Joyce. I like everything friendly and informal."

Tom said, "Well, Joyce it is. This isn't a pleasant event today. The building's gone, and three people are dead. The bodies are behind the screen. It's not pretty." He pointed to it, "and I knew them well. They were members of my church. In my mind, I can see them last Sunday with their hands held high praising the Lord. They may be in God's loving hands now, but there's a hole in my heart, a big hole."

Joyce looked at him. "I was a medic in the U. S. Army when we invaded Panama back in 1989. I've seen my share of death. You can't pretty it up. It's hard not to become callous."

Tom asked, "So how did you get from there to here?"

"After Panama, I decided I wanted something else than a nursing career. I used my G. I. Bill and went to journalism school at WVU. I took this job with Mr. Godfrey's paper in Cumberland a few months ago, and here I am today, covering a fire. Mr. Godfrey's showing me the ropes. He's been a great teacher and really knows his way around."

Mr. Godfrey quipped in, "Buttering up the boss will do you no good, but it is good to hear a compliment."

"No, really, Mr. Godfrey. If you were a jerk, I'd have told you so and quit. I've seen too many of those in my life so far. You've been nothing but helpful and a perfect gentleman. I couldn't ask for a better boss," she paused, "and please don't change."

They chuckled at the joke. A group of exhausted-looking firefighters came their direction. Tom got up and gave his chair to one of them as did several of the other people seated nearby. Tom and the other two walked away from the crowd, and Tom nearly ran into Cindy, owner of the restaurant in the burned-out building. Tears flowed down her face. "Cindy," Tom said. "I'm so sorry. There's nothing left."

She reached around and hugged him. "I know, Tom. I know. Tell me it'll be alright."

He hugged her back, "Somehow, Cindy, it'll be alright. I don't know how, but it'll be alright."

She hugged him tight for a moment and then let go. "Yeah, I keep holding on to that. I'll get through this somehow, but do you know the three Dowlens are dead? She was a great worker. I don't know who or how the funeral for them will be paid for."

"I'm wondering about that, too. The reason they ended up in Fort Ashby was they had little money after escaping persecution in the Middle East, and that went for the old car of theirs that died here, and there's none of their family in this country to help. I'll do the funeral for free, but there are a number of other expenses," he said.

Mr. Godfrey and Joyce Lynn listened discretely to the conversation. Mr. Godfrey spoke, "Joyce, we have a story here fit for the front page. Get some pictures, and I want you to talk with these two. Tell about how it affects her business and her personally. They both knew the deceased closely. This is a great human interest story." He paused. "Tom, you say these people were refugees with no relatives here in the USA and just getting by literally living hand to mouth." Tom nodded in agreement. "In times like these, my paper sometimes, as a public service, will start a fund for people, dead or alive, to help. I would like to start the fund with a check for $1,000. Do you think your church treasury could handle the donations? It would help the Dowlens funeral needs and give your church some needed publicity. What do you say? Do we have an agreement?"

Tom replied, "Sounds like a great idea to me. You'll need to make sure your readers know to put something to the effect like 'For the Dowlen Family Funeral' or similar on their checks they send. The church treasurer gets checks in the mail from our members when they're out of town. I want to keep everything on the up and up, and we need it the funds kept separate."

"Yes, I see your point. I will make certain that is included in the article. I will look over the final draft personally."

Tom said to Mr. Godfrey, "Thank you, sir. I thank you, and I'm sure if the Dowlens were here, they would overwhelm you with their thanks. I always expected behind that firm exterior, there beats a gentle heart that cared for people."

Mr. Godfrey was visibly surprised. "Tom," he said. "You have the rare gift of seeing into people. I know why you are a pastor."

It was now Tom's time to be ill at ease. "Mr. Godfrey, I'm just following Jesus's commands. "Love the Lord and love other people. It's as simple as that."

Mr. Godfrey nodded. "How often I have seen a complex situation have a very simple explanation which the so-called wise miss."

Tom said, "It looks like you also have a gift of insight, Mr. Godfrey."

He smiled slightly. "When you are in the business I am in, it pays to be able to read people."

The two men talked a little more until Joyce Lynn entered the group. She was finished taking pictures of the smoldering heaps and interviewing Cindy. She asked Tom some questions about the Dowlens. When this was over, he excused himself and began to work the crowd with Father Frank comforting and consoling anyone who needed it. The bottled water Tom brought came in handy and quenched the thirst of many. By two o'clock, only a few remained. Tom and the Padre left their vehicles parked where they were and walked across the road to The Talk of the Town Restaurant next to

Jay Heavner

the town memorial to the fallen in our nation's wars. It was late in the afternoon, and the lunch crowd was long gone. They took a secluded corner and told the waitress they wanted coffee, strong and black. Even though tired and hungry, they had much to talk about.

Chapter 19

The waitress named Wilma bought the men two cups of coffee and menus. They thanked her for the steaming beverages. She returned with a full pot, sat it down on the table, and said, "You guys look kinda tired and like you could use this. Been over at the fire?"

Padre replied, "Yes, we have, and it was a bad scene. Lots of hurting people over there."

"So I heard. Been here all day since early morning, dark 30. We sent coffee and donuts earlier and some sandwiches over for lunch. Lotta people been in here today. Cindy's breakfast crowd came over. Much as I liked the extra business, I hate to see something like this happen. It could have been this place just as easy." She paused. "I heard three people died, too."

Tom nodded, "Yes, I identified the bodies best I could. The two adults were the Dowlens, and the young girl looked like their daughter, but it was hard to tell she was so burned. Last time I saw anything like that was in Vietnam. Brought back some very unpleasant memories."

"I can believe it. Now I got your drinks, what do you want for lunch?"

Padre asked, "Could I still get breakfast? I missed it, and I've got a real hankerin' for some scrambled eggs and sausages?"

"I think so." She yelled to the cook in the kitchen. "Hey Charlie, can we still get breakfast for these hungry men? They were over at the fire and missed it."

Charlie looked up and made eye contact with Wilma. He looked at Padre and Tom and nodded. "Sure can."

"Okay, what'll it be?" she asked.

Padre spoke first. "I'm really starving. How about the number five? Two eggs over easy, bacon, a bagel, OJ, and grits."

"Sounds good. You do know the OJ costs extra?"

"That's fine."

"And for you?" she asked Tom.

"I'll take a number five too only make my eggs scrambled, no OJ, and home fries instead of grits."

"Sounds good," she said and took the two menus. "This shouldn't be too long. The lunch crowd has come and gone, but Charlie'll have to get the breakfast items out again for you guys. We'll put a rush on it." She turned and left the men with their coffee.

"What a day it's been," said Padre.

Tom jumped. His phone in his pocket vibrated from an incoming call. He clumsily reached for it and put it to his ear. "Hello?" He listened to the call. It was from Joann. "Yes, I'm okay. Padre and me are havin' breakfast in Fort Ashby."

"It's Joann," Tom said to Padre.

"Yes, the fire was as bad as we feared. The Dowlens died in the fire." Tom listened to her speak.

He said, "Yeah, it's terrible. They were good people who knew the Lord. How are things there?" Padre could hear the muted conversation, but not make it out. "Okay, things are good there and Doug's managing without me." Tom paused and listened some more. "Okay, great. I'll see you sometime before supper time. Bye. Love ya."

"Sounds like everything is hunky-dory on the home front," said Padre.

"They're getting along without me somehow," Tom chuckled. 'I'm glad we were here to help. Just sorry how this all played out. Three dead, businesses, and places people called home gone. Not a pretty picture. Life ain't always a bed of roses."

"I know where you're coming from. Consider the rose. Is it a rose bush with thorns or a thorn bush with roses?" said Padre.

"Let's skip that issue for now. Mr. Godfrey, the owner of the Cumberland newspaper, was here today, and he's willing to use his paper for a fundraiser to cover funeral expenses for the Dowlens. Their kin back home disowned them when they became Christians. They have no one here, and they barely were getting by as it was."

Padre replied," Yeah, I saw him and the cub reporter at the fire. He seems to have a hard exterior, but I guess you would need a thick skin for the business he's in. I think there's more to him than meets the eye."

"I believe you're right about that. I don't know exactly how the funeral arrangements will work out. Don't know who to contact on that. It'll work out somehow. It always does."

"You're right about that."

Tom said, "It's been a couple of weeks since we talked. How are things in your personal and professional life going?" Tom knew this would be a tough question for the Padre, but he needed to know.

"It's complicated." Tom waited for more. Padre began, "After I saw you that Monday at the restaurant in Cumberland, I drove the two-hour drive over to Pittsburgh. Everything was fine. Stacy was happy to see me, and we went for a walk in a local park. We talked about what to do. Were we making the right decision or not? Should we get married or not? While we were walking, Stacy had a sharp pain in her lower belly area. I could tell it hurt from the look on her face and the way she held her hand to her body. She wanted to go home, so we walked to the car. We drove for about two minutes, and she screamed in pain. She looked at me and pleaded, 'Take me to a hospital. I think I'm having a miscarriage.'"

Tom listened patiently, and the Padre continued, "I knew where the hospital was as we passed one on the way to the park. We got there quickly. Glad there wasn't any cops who saw my fancy driving." He gave a weak smile. "I drove up to the emergency entrance, and they took her right in. She was right. It was a miscarriage, and we lost the baby."

A tear ran down the big man's black cheek. "Brother," Tom asked. "Are you okay?"

"Give me a minute. I'll be alright." Padre wiped the tear from his eye. "She spent two days in the hospital. I think the doctor just wrote up some kind of female problem for the bill. That will keep her out of trouble with her employer. We both took the week off from work to recover. After I took her home from the hospital, we talked about what happened and what we should do now. I think we were both still in shock, but we decided to continue seeing each other and work it out. Right now, I'm not sure what'll happen. I want her as my wife, but things, like I said, have gotten complicated."

"I see what you mean. Can we pray on this?" Padre nodded his head. He held his two big hands across the table. Tom clasped them, and they both nodded their heads to pray. Tom began, "Almighty God, who knows all things; we come to you with heavy hearts today. My friend is going through some tough times, and he's not sure what to do, or how this will all turn out. Guide him as a good shepherd would his sheep. Strengthen him for what lies ahead, whatever it is."

Padre squeezed Tom's hands hard, and he began to speak, "Lord, you know all he said is true, and You know the whole story about what's going on in my life. I trust in You whatever the outcome and Lord, bless my brother Tom. I'm not the only one with problems. Lord, help all the hurting people in our community. That fire has affected a lot of lives and will for some time. And Lord, last but not least, we thank you for this food we are about to partake in. Amen."

"Amen," Tom echoed.

They released each other's hands and sat back in the booth. Wilma's voice called out from the other side of the empty restaurant. "You boys ready for that breakfast yet? It's ready, but I hated to interrupt your prayer meeting."

"Bring it on," Padre roared. "I could eat a whole pig, including the oink."

Wilma brought the food over to the table and said, "Well, you'll have to settle for this cooked bacon from Mr. Pig. Those oinks cook down to nothing' and ain't very nutritious. They don't stick to a man's ribs very well."

"We'll keep that in mind," said Tom. "Thank you. It looks good."

"It is good," she said, "and if you need anything else, holler. I'll be over yonder in the kitchen getting ready for the evening meal."

"Yeah, thanks from me, too. Do you have any ketchup for the eggs?" asked Father Frank.

Wilma smiled, "it's right there by the napkins."

"If it was a snake, it would have bite me," said the Padre.

"You keep them snakes to yourself. Don't need none in here," she said. "If there's anything else, just holler for me."

'We will," answered Tom, and the two hungry men dug into the warm meal.

They talked very little as they wolfed the meal down. When they finished, the Padre looked at Tom and asked, "And how's your life going? Have you heard anything more from than mysterious Voice character?"

Tom responded, "Overall, my life is going as well as can be expected. Business is good. Life with Joann and Miriah is good too, and as for The Voice guy, he hasn't contacted him lately, but I have this feeling he's close by, watching and waiting, bidding his time. I'll hear from him when he has something he needs to say. Oh, I did have another visit from the atheist who's been coming to my church."

Padre looked at him, "Isn't that like seeing a prostitute at a nunnery?"

"I see your point, but what better place for them? They can hear the Good News."

"So true. How'd it go? There's never enough evidence for scoffers. So many atheists I've met have been full of ridicule, intolerance, arrogance, and mockery, just the thing they say we do. Rather hypocritical."

"I've run across those, too. Mockery is never an argument. That's admitting defeat. No, I had none of that from Mr. Miller. Two things are playing in this for him. The first is the change for the better he has seen in his wife since she has become a Christian, and the second is he's getting old and wants to make sure he's got it right before he dies."

Padre nodded in agreement. "Yeah, some people deny the final curtain call is coming and get swept off the stage anyway, and others prepare for what comes next."

"He's seeking; I'll say that. He asked a lot of good questions. I don't mind dealing with someone who is honestly seeking."

"So what kind of questions and all did he ask?"

"A lot of questions about creation, design, and God's nature. He's having a hard time still believing the evolutionary line on how the universe has no design, purpose, no good or evil, only blind, pitiless indifference. It's left him feeling empty inside, especially when his eyes can see design everywhere. There's order in this world and universe. Even the simple cell is too complex just to happen. I think he's come to realize atheism is a faith itself in human intelligence. It believes everything is a product of a mindless, unguided process. If it's true though, how can you trust the thoughts from random firings of electrical impulses in the mind of evolved monkey brains? You know what C. S Lewis said on this?"

"C. S. Lewis? Didn't he write the *Chronicles of Narnia*?"

"That's the guy. He said, 'If our minds are wholly dependent on brains, our brains on biochemistry and biochemistry on the meaningless flux of atoms, I can't understand how the thoughts of those minds should have any more significance than the sound of the blowing winds."

Padre smiled, "He said it much better than you did."

Tom grimaced. "You really know how to make a guy feel wanted."

"You know me well enough to know when I'm pulling your leg, my friend. Those were some good questions that atheist was asking," said Father Frank. "Sounds to me like he's coming over from the dark side."

"I believe it's just a matter of time before he convinces himself of what he already knows. He's noticed how many of the scientists in the past were Christians and how scientifically accurate the Bible is. It's never been wrong from an archaeological perspective. How could it not be true with all the fulfilled prophecy?"

"Yeah, I believe you're right. He's convincing himself."

"Believe it or not, he did most of the talking and convincing. He even quoted Werner von Braun, a man I have met twice, but that's another story. He said, 'One cannot be exposed to the law and order in the universe without concluding there must be design and purpose behind it all. The better we understand the universe and all it harbors, the more reason we have found to marvel at the inherent design upon which it is based.' I sat there, nodded my head, and just gave a point here and there. He said as a man of science; he also had a hard time when he saw no evidence of evolution in the fossil records and how all physical laws support special creation."

The Padre added, "Sounds to me like he's realized wishing God does not exist does not make it so. Just because you don't want to believe in God does not make there not be one."

Tom said, "I think it's only a matter of time before he admits what he already knows. There is a God, and he needs to be right with Him. I believe he'll make the right decision soon. It may be a Sunday when he's at church with his wife, or it could be just as easy as sitting on his couch in his living room. A man can get right with God wherever he is. It can be a pauper's shack or a mansion, on a beach, or in a prison. God's there waiting. Jesus said, 'I stand at the door and knock. Open the door, and I will enter.' He's ready whenever they are."

"Preach on brother. I'm starting to get glory bumps all over me."

Tom laughed at that. "Amen to that. Hey, I think we better get moving. I have things that I let slide for this, and I know you did, too."

"You're right on that. We better go," said the Padre.

They left a generous tip for Wilma and paid their bill at the counter. Wilma took their money and said, "Everything was good, right?"

Tom and Padre looked at each other and nodded. "Yeah, it was good and tasty."

Wilma said, "That's good, but you guys ate it so fast I wasn't sure you tasted it or not. Come again."

"I believe we will," replied the Padre.

Tom took the change. It had been his turn to pay the bill. They left the building and walked the short distance to where their cars were parked behind the danger tape. The Deputy recognized them and waved them through.

As they were getting ready to separate, the Padre said, "Keep me in your prayers. I'm gonna need it."

"Yeah," Tom said. "Me, too. It ain't over till the fat lady sings, and I'm not sure she's even warming up. Keep in touch. See ya."

"Will do. You do the same."

The two men got into their separate cars and drove away. Father Frank headed north on WV Highway 28, but Tom turned down Dans Run Road. There was something he needed to do. He drove the short distance past the Methodist Church and the Community Building across the street where his small congregation met on Sunday. In his mind's eye, he could see the Dowlen family, all three of them, walking up the steps again. He and many others were going to miss them. Tom drove over the small bridge and a short distance further until he was at the Old Fort. He chuckled to himself as he thought of a humorous story a lady had told him about the Fort. She cut the grass out front when she was a teenager, and she was afraid to cut around the back because of the stories about the ghost back there. Her friend said she wasn't afraid of no ghost, took the mower, and began to cut around the back. The first girl was rather mischievous, and with the mower's loud roar masking her approach, she snuck up behind her friend and put her hand on the second girl's shoulder. She let out a scream that would wake the dead. He had some friends like that, too.

He took a right, passed the elementary school on his left, and ascended the hill the Fort Ashby Cemetery was on. It was said to be an Indian burial ground before the white settlers starting using it to bury their dead also. He didn't know if it was true, but he did know for over 200 years the town had placed its dearly departed here, including his son.

He pulled up to the parking area and saw the caretaker, Jenny, riding her mower in the upper section. He waved, and she waved back. They'd known each other for a long time. Another noise behind him got his attention. Jenny's daughter, Leah, was busy with a weed eater around the older, above-ground monuments. Tom grabbed his hat from the truck and found a plastic chair someone left at the little pavilion. He took it and walked up to his son's grave. He walked past so many graves with familiar names: Dohrman, Weaver, Miller, Adams, Long, and others. *Seems like no matter how much money or how much fame we have on this Earth, we all end up in a plot like this,* he thought.

He placed the chair next to the grave marker that read "Brian Kenney" and sat down. Tom thought for a moment and began to speak, "You know, Brian, I miss you. You're gone from this earth, but we here remember you. I wish things could have been different. Life's not fair, and sometimes people leave too soon." A tear rolled down his cheek as his eyes watered. "I just came from the square uptown. The old block building burned to the ground, and three people died. Would you tell them I miss them, too? Oh, Brian, life can be so short. Someday, in the not so distant future, my ole body will be here, too, but I'll be with you and my Lord and the ones I love." He wanted to say more, but tears filled his eyes. He choked up and began to cry. Tears fell like rain on Brian's grave as Tom's pain left his body. He wiped the tears from his eyes and blew his watery nose into a handkerchief. Tom looked down at the grave. "I really miss you, son, and know we'll be together soon in a better place. Till then, remember, I love you."

Tom stood up and began walking away, carrying the borrowed chair. He placed it where he found it and got in the truck. *You never know when it's your time to go.* He put the truck in gear and started down the hill out of the cemetery. Life is full of surprises. You never know what is around the corner, but he did know he would be called on to perform a funeral for three people who died and he had better start preparing. *Oh Lord, give me the strength to carry on. You always do no matter what comes my way. You are my strength, my shield, and my strong tower. You are my fortress when I am weak. I couldn't make it a day without you. Amen.*

Jay Heavner

Chapter 20

The outpouring of support for the Dowlen family from the tri-state area and beyond overwhelmed Tom and the members of his small church. Not only had Mr. Godfrey placed the story on the front page of the *Cumberland Times-News*, but it had also been picked up by the wire services and gone nationwide. Tom suspected Mr. Godfrey pulled some strings to see this happened. Much more than enough money for proper caskets, funeral arrangements, burial sites, and other necessities came in. The Fort Ashby Lions Club offered to donate land for three side by side graves in the new section, but with plenty of funds available, the sites were purchased from the organization.

After the coroner released the bodies, Upchurch Funeral Home prepared and kept them for the wake on Friday afternoon and evening. There would be no viewing for obvious reasons. Tom and the Padre were present on Friday to comfort the mourners. Father Frank dressed in his usual Sunday robes, and Tom wore a dark suit, white shirt, and red tie, something he rarely did as Sunday services at his church were informal. He discovered his shirt was tight around the neck, and he made a mental note to either get a bigger shirt or lose some weight. Joann's good cooking showed on him.

The crowd was so large the police were called to direct traffic. Some of the local men were temporally deputized to help. The parking lot of the funeral home was full, and the excess cars parked wherever space could be found. Most went to the parking lot by the Custard Stand at the town square in front of the burned out building's ruins. It remained a grim reminder of the tragedy that had happened.

Tom and the Padre were blown away by the people who came, young and old. Many shared stories about the Dowlen family Tom had never heard. He only wished he'd known these accolades when they were alive. Funerals are challenging times for pastors. Death always brings stress. Sometimes it was difficult to find the right words when a vile person died, or when a tragedy occurred. It was not easy to find kind words for a person of bad reputation, or when lives were taken unexpectedly and too soon.

Tom felt exhausted but also pleased at the display of support by the community. He slept well that night. Tomorrow, he'd give the final service for the Dowlens at the little pavilion in the cemetery, and he knew what to say.

Tom was up at the break of dawn Saturday; even so, he could smell bacon frying. *Joann must already be up and fixin' breakfast.* Tom grabbed a WVU Football T-shirt, sweat pants, and with sleep still in his eyes, made his way to the kitchen. Joann saw him and said, "Hi, honey. You looked so peaceful laying in our bed; I left you sleeping. You've got a big day ahead."

Tom yawned and stretched. "Yeah, sure do. It's always hard to say goodbye to friends even though we believe they're in a better place with the Lord, and we'll see them again. I think we grieve for our loss, not their gain."

"Yes, I believe you're right, Tom. This tragedy seems to be bringing out the best in the community."

Tom nodded, "Yeah, the outpouring of support, both emotional and financial, has been hard to believe. I want to mention this when I give the eulogy for the Dowlen family. I smell coffee. Can I have some?"

"I'm kind of busy with the eggs now, Tom. I swear; I wait on you hand and foot, and you still don't know how to get the coffee."

Tom got up, went behind Joann at the stove, and began to nibble on her neck as he held his hands on her arms.

"Tom," she pleaded, and part demanded. "Stop that, or I'll whack you into next Sunday. I'm busy."

Jay Heavner

"Okay honey, you know a woman at a stove is a turn on for us guys."

She rolled her eyes. "Yes, I know. A man's stomach is the way to his heart."

"Well, one of the two popular ways," he said.

"Tom, you're a pain, but I love you just the same. Now, get your own coffee. It's your favorite, Chock Full 'O Nuts. The eggs will be done in a minute. Get the bagels in the toaster, okay?"

"Sure thing. Ain't nothin' says love to a man's heart like a good breakfast and coffee. Say, that would be a good title for a book, 'Nothing Says Love like Breakfast in the Morning.' with the subtitle, 'A Man's Point of View.'"

Joann again rolled her eyes, "Tom, there are days I wonder about you. Who is this stranger I married?"

Tom laughed, "You know what they say, 'when the goin' gets weird, the weird get goin.'"

"Tom, I'd send you back to your mother if I could."

"Not a chance on that. Number one, she wouldn't take me and Number 2, you know as well as I do, she died decades ago, and I still miss her. It seems like yesterday, Dad and I stood by her new grave over at the cemetery outside of Cumberland. I need to go soon and put some flowers on her and Dad's graves."

Tom poured his coffee and a cup for Joann, too. When he made it back to the table, two plates of eggs with bacon were waiting. He went to the toaster for the bagels, grabbed them with his fingers, and burnt them slightly. After blowing a comforting breath on the fingers, he gave one bagel to her and kept the other for himself. She spread cream cheese on hers, and he covered his with some blackberry jam purchased from Wayne's Grocery. It was a new product from a local producer. Wayne had always tried to help the little guy. Tom remembered how he'd started and will never forget Wayne's help in his business's beginning, even though it was a little reluctant.

Tom blessed the meal, and the hungry couple chowed down. They were much too busy feeding their faces for small talk other than, "pass the salt and pepper," or "this is good," and one "thank you."

Tom helped Joann clean up after they finished, and she made a plate for Miriah when she awoke.

Tom asked, "Are you gonna be able to make the service at the cemetery at 11:00? I'd really like you to be there."

She said, "I'll do what I can. I'm helping prepare the food with the ladies of the church for the reception after the funeral. Thank God, Padre let us use the kitchen and fellowship hall at his church."

"Good ole Padre comes through in a pinch as usual. The man has a heart as big as he is," he said. "Gonna be a lot of hungry people after the services. Are you bringing Miriah? She could help."

"I want to, but she is kind of queasy on this. Ruhama was a friend, and she's not used to seeing someone that young die."

"I know where you are coming from, but I think she needs to realize death can come at any age. She knows about the Lord and what we need to do for salvation. I know it's a heavy dose of reality, but life is like that. It's not always pretty."

"You're right. I'll see if I can convince her. If not, I'll leave her with my sister, okay?"

"Do what you can. I'd like to see you both at the funeral."

Joann nodded yes to Tom. He left the kitchen, walked outside, and headed to the warehouse for a quick look-see. No one was working today, and everything was in order. Nacho looked up from the barnyard at his owner and went back to grazing. His dogs lay sleeping beside a tree nearby. *Tragedy or not, the world keeps spinning*, he thought.

He walked back to the house and went inside. Miriah was eating the food her mother prepared. "Hi, Daddy, you're up," she said.

"Yes, it's Saturday, but it's gonna be a busy day with the funeral and reception afterward," Tom said. Miriah dropped her eyes to her plate. "I'd like you to be there. Ruhama was your friend."

"I know, Daddy. Why did she have to die?"

"I wish I knew. There's a time to be born and a time to die. No one knows when it will happen, but someday it will. I've had several close visits from the death angel myself. We'll want to remember Ruhama and keep the memories of her alive, okay?"

A tear rolled down her cheek. "I'll try, Daddy. I'll try."

Tom said, "And I'd like you to be at the services today with your Mom. I believe Ruhama would want you to attend."

She sniffed and wiped away a tear. "Okay, Daddy. I'll try."

"That's my girl." Tom bent over and kissed her on the top of the head. "Now, I have to get ready and go, or I'll be late for the funeral myself, and I think they'll notice if I'm late."

"Okay, Daddy. Love you."

"Love you too, sugar."

"Sugar? Daddy, that's what you call Nacho."

"Well, I love you both and mommy, too."

"Mommy says you're rotten and I agree, and I bet some of those brays Nacho makes are saying 'you're rotten, too.'"

"Looks like I'm busted. You guys know me too well. I have to go and get my rotten self ready. See you later, alligator."

She smiled, "In a while, crocodile."

Tom headed up the stairs to the bedroom, found his one good suit he rarely wore, and put it on. *Well, surprise, surprise. Someone shined his black dress shoes. The doer of this mysterious good deed had to be identified and rewarded.* He would round up the usual suspects for questioning just as they did in the old movie "Casa Blanca." Someone needed to be thanked for actions above and beyond the call of duty.

He combed his hair, which seemed to grow grayer daily. No one had called him a spring chicken for a long time. Tom walked down the steps, found Joann in the kitchen, kissed her goodbye, and was out the door. His old Chevy pickup sat waiting and proudly displayed on the back window, was a new WV Mountaineers sticker.

Traffic on WV Route 28 was light as he drove to Fort Ashby. *Bet ole George Washington would sure be surprised to see how this road and area look now. The old buffalo trail, little more than a trace, was a two-lane paved road, and the old barren wilderness was populated by lots of people and their homes. He'd be pleased,* Tom thought.

He drove by the Catholic Church and saw several familiar cars at the Fellowship Hall. *Looks like the Calvary Chapel people in the congregation were busy preparing the reception meal for after the services.* Padre walked between the buildings and Tom tooted his horn. Father Frank looked toward the sound, recognized the old truck, smiled and waved in return. *Where would we be without friends? A man with a true friend is rich, while one who only has only gold is poor.*

He traveled by the old barn at Siple's Curve with the Sinclair Dinosaur painted on one side and a Mail Pouch Tobacco advertisement on the other. The pungent smell of fresh manure filled his nose — n*othing like the scent of fresh, green grass cow pies.* Memories of youthful adventure and stupidity came to mind. He and another boy decided it would be great fun to chase some cows captive in a barnyard which, unknown to them, were full of lubricating fresh, spring grass. The Irish talk about the wearing of the green, but it wasn't quite the same for the boys that day. They chased the cows, but the bovines had the last laugh. They turned and ran from the boys and a disgusting half liquid-half solid substance shot from the rear ends of the cows and coated the boys. Once was enough for him. Common sense came easy for this country boy.

Over the bridge across Patterson Creek, he drove, took the long sweeping turn at the fairgrounds, and continued on through the sleepy, little town. He turned right into the parking lot at the Upchurch Funeral Home and found a place to park. Bright red, highly polished fire trucks from the Fort Ashby and Short Gap Volunteer Fire Departments, as well as a lime green truck from Patterson Creek VFD, were parked ready to carry the three caskets to the nearby cemetery. Tom would ride in the first truck driven by a man named Leroy who'd gone to school with him.

Tom walked into the building and was greeted by the owner. It was not the first time they had met, and it would not be the last. It seemed like their businesses were similar; they both served the living and the dead. They spoke on the arrangements for the trip to the cemetery and the services. All seemed in order. Tom talked to some of the waiting firemen who told him of coffee and donuts in the next room, which they were wolfing down. Everyone was invited for a reception afterward at the Catholic Church.

At 10:30, the three heavy caskets were lovingly and gently carried by six formally dressed firemen from the building to the waiting three fire trucks with turned-on flashing red lights. The caskets were securely strapped down for their final journey. In a few minutes, the three trucks pulled out onto WV Route 28 with an escorted by a Mineral County Sheriff's Department vehicle leading the way with blue lights beaming. A state trooper blocked traffic coming from Springfield at the one and only traffic light in town. The caravan made a left onto Dans Run Road, and it was lined with people carrying American flags of every size, large, medium, and small. Slowly they proceeded by the Fort Ashby VFD building, the Methodist Church, and stopped in the road in front of the Community Building, where the Dowlens had attended church. At that point, all three fire trucks turned on their loud sirens to honor the fallen family. From Tom's perch in the lead truck, he could see children covering their ears from the tumult. They continued, sounding for a full minute and abruptly stopped. *There was no way the Lord could not notice the people of this little town were bringing His three children home to Him.*

The three trucks resumed their travel and made a right at Ashby's Old Fort from which the town took its name. They did the best they could to avoid numerous potholes in the road by the elementary school. The trucks continued up the steep road past the old section of the graveyard. At the top of the knoll, they turned right and stopped at the small pavilion. Air brakes activated with a hiss, and the engines turned off. Men who rode on the side of the trucks dismounted, took the straps off the caskets, and gently carried them to sturdy racks where each was placed side by side. Tom motioned to the crowd of people standing behind the open building to come forward, which they did. He noted Joann and Miriah in the crowd. Mr. Logan Dalton, from the funeral home, handed him a microphone, and Tom began to speak.

"I'm very pleased you took time from your busy schedules to be here today. I'm sure the Dowlens would be surprised and maybe a little embarrassed. They were not people who wanted to draw attention to themselves. I knew them as their pastor. They showed up one Sunday morning dressed in the best clothes they owned. Most of you know they were refugees from religious persecution in the Middle East. The old car they had broke down here in Fort Ashby, and they decided this was where they belonged. Mr. Dowlen did whatever he could find for work before the school hired him as a custodian, and he kept the school spotless. I remember him telling me how he was glad to have a job and as the Bible says, he did his work as unto the Lord. He was saving for another car but never could get enough for a replacement. Seemed like the money was always needed someplace else, new shoes, doctor bills, or some other unexpected expense. I think we can all relate to that."

A little laugh rippled through the crowd. "It was hard to understand him sometimes with his broken English. I know he had a lot he could have complained about, but I rarely ever saw him downtrodden in spite of his circumstances. When I asked him how he did it, he looked at me a little shocked and said, 'Pastor, the Good Book says, take it all to the Lord and I do. You know that.' He was so right. That day he ministered to me when I needed it. He loved humor and could tell many jokes. One I remember well, I'll share it with you now. Seemed a Priest was retiring after twenty years in his parish. The senior State Senator from the area was to give a little speech at the retirement event. He was late, so the priest decided to say his own words while they waited for his arrival.

He started, "I'm so glad for a sense of humor. My very first impression of this parish was from the first confession I heard here. I believed I had been assigned to a horrible place. This person entered my confessional and told me took a TV and lied about it to the police to get off. He'd stolen money, embezzled from his employer, cheated on his wife with women and men, done illegal drugs, and several other things worse than that I shall not mention. As the days went on, I learned my people in the parish weren't like that at all. Indeed, I really did have a great congregation full of good and loving people."

Jay Heavner

As the Priest finished his speech, the politician arrived full of apologies for being late. He went to the platform and immediately began his presentation. He said, "I'll never forget the day our parish Priest arrived. As a matter of fact, I had the honor of being the first person he heard a confession from."

Laughter erupted from the crowd, and when it had quieted, Tom said, "That was the kind of man Elias Dowlen was, always ready to give a dependable helping hand and quick with a smile and a joke. I was glad to be his pastor and call him my friend.

"Hannah Dowlen was the glue holding this struggling family together. She was the first to find a job in Fort Ashby. She went to work as a cook at Cindy's Restaurant in the building where she lived. I knew Mr. Dowlen better than I knew the Missus. Her English was not the best, and I had trouble understanding her often. I saw Cindy at the funeral parlor last night, and she filled me in on some details on her. Cindy at first was a little afraid to hire her with the communication problem, but she offered to work for two days for free as a trial period. How could she refuse an offer like that? At noon on the second day, Cindy hired her and paid her for the two days. It was only later she learned the family was down to nothing and had been eating rice and beans and nothing else for the last two weeks. She was such a good worker; Cindy only wished she could afford to pay her more. It was Hannah Dowlen that introduced shawarmas and falafels to this traditional meat and potatoes community. Cindy said once people tried them, they came back for more and usually brought a friend along. One day Hannah wasn't feeling well, and Cindy had asked her what was wrong. She said she'd been beaten by a mob of men one day in the old country who did not like Christians. Cindy told her she could rest and leave, but she insisted on staying and doing her job. She was one you could depend upon.

"And what of young Ruhama? I saw her smiling face at church every Sunday. Most of what I know comes from what the kids from church and school told me about her. She spoke Arabic and English fluently and was at the top of her class in Spanish. She had her whole life ahead of her, but she was taken way too soon. One of her classmates told me she confided in him that she had a brother who was killed because the family was Christian. They never told me of this terrible part of their past lives.

"This young lady will be missed by all who knew her in the short time she was here. I don't know why tragedies like this happen; we only know they do in this fallen world. One thing I do know for sure, Jesus Christ told us He overcame death and the grave. The Dowlen family followed the Lord, and we know we will see them again." Several amens could be heard coming from the crowd. "They'd want me to tell you that you can have the same assurance of life after death with the Lord in Heaven if you will just give your life to Jesus today. I give you that opportunity. Come talk with me or with any of the town's pastors. They'll be more than happy to help. Thank you for coming. The Dowlens would not have been able to believe how this community and area came together for them. I would like to thank the Volunteer Firemen of Fort Ashby, Short Gap, and Patterson Creek for being pallbearers, and I believe I saw Mr. Godfrey of the *Cumberland Times-News* newspaper standing in the back of the crowd. I especially thank him for all he has generously done in telling the Tri-state area and beyond of this families' plight. We could not have succeeded without his help." A gentle applause came from the crowd. "To the Dowlen family, may you rest in peace until we see you again. And to all the living, I give you these verses from the book of Numbers in the Old Testament: May the Lord bless you and keep you. May His face shine upon you and be gracious unto you. May He turn His face to you and give you peace. Amen."

Many amens were heard from the crowd. Some left quickly, but others stayed around to talk. The Firemen went to their trucks and quickly left. A call had come in of a bad wreck on WV Route 28 near the top of Middle Ridge. Springfield VFD was requesting assistance.

Several people complimented Tom on the eulogy, but he was looking for Joann and Miriah. A hand touched his shoulder, and he turned to see his wife and daughter. "We made it," Joann said. "A little late, but we made it. We had to park at the school and walk up here."

"I'm glad you made it. The weather cooperated for us." He looked toward the west. "This had got to be one of the prettiest sights on the earth, such beauty among the ashes here."

Joann said, "Yes, it is. Maybe one day this will be our final resting place, too."

Tom felt a tug on his shirt. It was Miriah trying to get his attention. "What is it, honey? What do you want?"

"Daddy, I want what you and Mommy and the Dowlens have. I want to become a Christian today."

"Oh honey, that's wonderful. Joann, let's pray." Tom got down on his knees next to Miriah, as did Joann. "Lord, you heard what this young lady said. She wants to become a Christian. I know she knows what this means from all the preachin' and teachin' 'bout You she's heard in her life. You forgive our sins when we ask. You'll be our constant guide and friend. You said You would never forget or forsake us. She wants to be one of Your children today. Just take her as she is. Amen." And they all said amen.

Tom hugged Miriah and said, "Today, you are a new creation in Jesus Christ."

She smiled. 'You know Daddy; I feel different…so..so…clean."

"Your sins are gone. That's why."

"Yeah," she said. "I feel good all over." She paused. "Daddy, do you think my friend Ruhama and her family know?"

"I think so. Yes, I think they do."

Joann spoke to her, "I'm so happy for you. You've made my day. I really hate to stop this celebration of new life, but there's a bunch of people expecting a lunch at Padre's church. We better get going."

They walked down the hill to the school. *What a day it had been,* thought Tom. First, the services for the Dowlens and now his daughter becoming a Christian. He remembered a proverb an old Jewish man had told him, 'Out of every bad thing, something good can come' and he would know—he'd survived one of history's darkest times, the Holocaust. *May it never happen again,* but Tom feared it would. *Each generation seems to think it's smarter than the previous and then sadly repeats the same mistakes. Without the Lord,* Tom thought, *all this would be very depressing. What would I do?*

Jay Heavner

Chapter 21

TGIF! Tom was happy, happy, happy to see it finally arrive. Like the people at Knobley Mountain Bottled Water Company, he was glad when the weekend rolled around. The week had been super busy for all as the sales volume continued to climb, and Tom was taking up the slack as usual. He'd helped rearrange routes to fit the new normal. All routes had grown too large for one man, so a little was sliced off each for a new route Tom was developing and working this week.

He breathed a sigh of relief when the last truck came in late Friday afternoon. The driver, Jared, quickly filled out his weekly paper report and left. Doug, his son, needed to leave a little early, so Tom closed up the shop. It seemed he had a dinner date with a young lady he met at the Cumberland Soaring Club. All too well, Tom remembered the ups and downs of young love. He hoped all went well, and Doug remembered his table manners, not one of his strong points.

Tom locked up the warehouse and headed for his house's back door, which opened into the kitchen. Typically, Joann had a great Friday evening meal set for the two of them and her daughter Miriah, but nothing had been done. The table wasn't even set. *Joann's been awful moody this week, but sometimes women are like that.* He looked around the house, but she was not inside. He located her in the old swing on the porch. He sat down beside her, but she said nothing. They swung gently back and forth for a while, and then she spoke, "Honey, we need to talk."

Nothing brings fear to a man's heart more than the words 'Honey, we need to talk,' and Tom was no exception in the masculine world. His mind kicked into overdrive. *Had she wrecked the car, or ran up their credit card? Was Miriah sick or had someone seen him talking friendly with a woman or female manager at one of the stores and put a bug in her ear about him maybe having an affair? What could it be?*

"Honey, I have a confession to make to you."

Well, at least he was off the hook, but what could it be?

"You know we've been wanting to add to our family, so on Monday, I went in for a complete physical. I've not had one for years, and I wanted to know everything was in good order. The general practitioner did not like what she saw and recommended I see an OB/GYN specialist. I was lucky they had a cancellation today, and they got me in." She took a long pause. "What they found wasn't good. They said it was very, very unlikely I could ever become pregnant again."

Tom said, "That's disappointing, but there are specialists that can help with that problem."

Joann lowered her eyes, and a tear rolled down her cheek. "It's not that, Tom. A specialist won't help." He looked at her, puzzled. "Tom, I've been keeping a secret from you. You know how my first husband walked out on me and to this day, we still do not know where he is."

Tom nodded.

"I was left with all the bills. He wiped out our checking and savings accounts and ran up every credit card we had to the max. I didn't know how I'd provide for myself, let along Miriah. About that time, I found out I was pregnant. The whole world seemed to be weighed down on my shoulders. I turned to a 'friend,' and she advised me to have an abortion. She knew of a place in Baltimore that would quietly 'take care of things.' They did alright. They did such a 'good job,' it now looks like I'll never be able to have any more children. The doctors said they'd never seen a job that bad. Tom, I've regretted my decision every day of my life since. I wanted you so bad as a husband. I prayed for one like you. God blessed me, warts and all, with you. I was so afraid of what you would think of me for doing this, and I was worried for you. What would the people at your church say if they knew the pastor's wife had an abortion? Oh, Tom, I'm so sorry. I've made such a mess of things. Can you ever forgive me?"

Tom was stunned. It seemed his rock he leaned on in time of troubles was now a lump of clay. He put his arms around her, and she began to cry. The crying became sobbing, and tears fell like rain. Her body shook as she wept. Tom knew laments like this. Commonly, they occur at funerals when people mourned for their loss, and she was in sorrow for her losses, her lost child and now her barrenness. He held her close, and the tears wash away the pain as she cried. The sobbing stopped, and she laid her head on Tom's shoulder. Joann wiped away the tears from her eyes and on her face and sniffled through her nose. She pulled away from him and asked in a small voice, "Can you forgive me, Tom?" Her eyes begged for an answer.

"Joann, I will love you no matter what. I took you for better or worse, for richer or poorer, in sickness and in health. I forgive you for hiding the complete truth from me. If I'd been in your shoes, I probably would have done the same. I still love this gift God gave me, and I know that He has forgiven you also."

"Tom, I don't deserve you."

Tom's face turned a mixture of grimace and grin. "Nor I you."

The couple sat on the swing and rocked silently for the longest of time. They held each other close in their arms, but a rude noise disturbed the stillness. Tom's stomach growled. "Mercy," said Joann. "We need to take care of that before it eats your backbone, and I don't have a thing cooked."

"How about fish and chips at Linda's? It's Friday, you know. It should be her special of the day," said Tom.

"Sounds great to me. I'm buying, and I won't take no for an answer," she replied.

"You're on. One more thing. We need to pray about this."

"Okay," Joann said with some question in her voice.

Tom held her close and began. "Dear Father, most wonderful Creator and Counselor. You know all that just happened here. You know everything. If it be Your will, please give us a child just as you opened the womb of Your maidservant Hannah in ancient times. If the answer is no, help us accept it. Either way, we know You are good. Amen."

Joann let out a deep breath. "Amen."

They sat on the swing a little longer, and Tom's stomach growled again, this time louder.

Joann said, "Let's get going before that thing eats us both up. I need to go upstairs and grab a jacket. Oh, I forgot to tell you. Miriah is staying with her cousins at my sister's house tonight. I'll be right back," and off she went.

Tom continued to swing. Life was always full of surprises. Things never seemed settled. Tom prayed to himself, "Dear God, help me to live that prayer. I need you so."

Joann came back on the porch with a jacket on. "Ready? I could eat a whale."

"Think Linda has halibut or whiting. You may want to check with Captain Ahab for the whale."

"You know, Tom. I love you."

"And I love you." His stomach growled loudly once more. "Saints preserve us. Let's get supper before this thing doth consume us both." They did. And it was good as it always was at Linda's.

Jay Heavner

Chapter 22

Six months ago, strong man Big Tony was transferred from the prison in Frederick, Maryland, to the Western Maryland Correctional Institute. His 'job' at the former prison was to recruit members for the Voice's criminal operations mainly in the state of Maryland and also to bring peace among the different groups at the facility. He'd done his job well, and The Voice needed his expertise in the new prison near Cumberland, Maryland. The Voice had many connections in the state's political arena, which pulled strings and had him relocated. Big Tony's 'job' was to do the same at this violent place. The Warden would have what he wanted, no more reports in the papers of killings of guards or inmates, and The Voice would have what he wanted, more recruits for his purposes. It was a win-win situation for all, something the Voice always sought. Happy people kept their tongues still.

It was not easy, but the Warden looked the other way, and Big Tony developed his own organization with snitches and enforcers. Obey the group's rules, and things went well for you. If you disobeyed, an enforcer used intimidation. If the inmate was stubborn or stuck on stupid, a beating and some time in solitary came next. Most prisoners could see the writing on the prison wall and got the idea quickly. Reports of violence went down rapidly, and the papers soon went off to other stories.

Politicians and bureaucrats like to claim there never was enough money. More money means more power for them. Money had been appropriated for more facilities at the prison, but it was short of what was needed when hidden kickbacks were quietly taken out. Big Tony saw an opportunity and had a solution to this problem. One thing the prison did have, lots of idle hands looking for something to do. Big Tony knew many of the men possessed construction skills, and he created a plan together with the Warden. They had enough money for building materials and blueprints, but little else. Big Tony and men he selected would oversee the construction of new facilities, and trusted inmates were to provide the labor. In return for the work, the Warden would look the other way when alcohol and drugs were brought to reward the workers. The word spread throughout the prison and craftsmen of all trades came out of the woodwork. Laborers, carpenters, electricians, equipment operators and plumbers all indicated their willingness to cooperate under these conditions.

All site preparation was done by hand. Large amounts of earth typically moved by machinery were moved by human labor as done in third world countries. A small hill was leveled, deep footers were dug for the foundation, and excess earth was dumped where Warrior Creek entered the Potomac River. The land where the prison sat had been the site of an old French and Indian War fort, several grist mills on Warrior Run, numerous old homesteads, and until recently, the Celanese Fibers Corporation manufacturing facility. The state of Maryland acquired the site when the company was declared bankrupt. Large amounts of refuse and debris from years of human activity were dug up by the inmate workers and dumped down by the river. Celanese buried many obsolete pieces of machinery over the years of operation which the workers found. Among the refuse uncovered was a rusted and ancient piece of weighty metal resembling a pipe. It was about 3 feet long and had a hard, old wooden plug forced in one end. This too, was moved to the trash dump down by the river.

The project was slowly completed by the inmates who did not want it to end, but it was finished just the same. Completion meant the end of the good times. The Warden put in a good word for certain inmates who had time knocked off their sentences. The Governor and other elected officials praised him for his "innovative and creative solutions to financial challenges with funding for the facility." It had been a win-win situation for all as long as certain details were overlooked, and all were willing to turn a blind eye to get the new buildings done.

The Warden encouraged the inmates to show up for Bible studies. This looked good on his reports when attendance went up, not that he cared about what went on, nor did most of the inmates who saw it as a safe place to let their guard down and relax awhile. But there had been some surprises. Big Tony liked to check out the group of men that felt "called by the Lord" to prison ministry. There was every flavor of denomination present from Baptist and Buddhist to Zoroaster and everything in between. The two he liked best were a salt and pepper team, Pastor Tom and Padre Frank. One or the other was always present on Thursday evening, sometimes both. And the two he disliked most were the same salt and pepper team. The black man looked like he should be playing the front line for a professional football team. He was not one to mess with. The other man was average in every way imaginable. What bothered Big Tony and some of the other inmates was that both preached Jesus Christ crucified, all men were sinners, and He was the only way of salvation.

Many men would try to upset Pastor Tom while he was preaching. You could tell it irritated him, but he simply continued. No one gave Padre Frank any grief. That face's eyes could turn from love to daggers in a split second, and no one did it more than once.

One evening, when the commons area was packed with inmates for Bible study, and Pastor Tom was alone, the inmates tormented him without mercy. They wanted to break him. Big Tony led the verbal attack while the amused guards looked on, and he would never forget what happened. After the numerous taunts, Big Tony stood to his feet and sneered, "Little man, you got no balls."

The room roared with laughter. Pastor Tom stood and stared intently at the standing big man. He said nothing and continued to stare. The laughter died slowly, and the room grew quiet as a tomb. All could see Pastor Tom was mad, and they waited to see what he would do. Calmly, he walked to Big Tony and looked hard into the large man's eyes. Big Tony winked one eye at the guards who stayed in their position to the left. He turned back and down into the smaller man's eyes. Pastor Tom spoke forcefully, "I left one of my balls on a battlefield in Vietnam at a place called Ia Drang. Ever hear of it? Many good men died in those three days of hell, and I was one of the lucky ones who survived. Hundreds came back home in body bags."

A hush went through the crowded commons. One man coughed, and the guards stirred nervously. *Ia Drang*, Big Tony remembered that name. He'd been a medic in Vietnam and worked triage for causalities the choppers brought in. *Ia Drang*, now he remembered. That face staring at him was familiar. Now he recalled that hurting, blood-covered soldier as he was years ago who asked about his Indian friend. Big Tony lied to him and said the Indian would make it, but he knew he was already dead. This was the same man he treated on the last day of the terrible carnage.

Big Tony stared at the man standing before him. His face became a smile, and he said, "Any man who served his country on a bloody battlefield is a man I can respect. Preacher, preach on. We want to hear what you got to say."

A buzz went through the inmates, and the guards breathed a sigh of relief. Pastor Tom walked back to the front and began to preach. He spoke for twenty minutes, and the inmates hung on to every word. At the end, he asked who would be the first to take a courageous step forward, repent of his sins and accept Jesus Christ as savior and Lord.

Ten men did. Big Tony was not one of them, but he never forgot that night. No one gave Pastor Tom grief anymore—Big Tony made sure of it. Though Pastor Tom never knew, he was under Big Tony's protection while he was at the prison. A snitch a month later informed him that Looney Louie hated Pastor Tom for his bold preaching and was going to run a shiv in him during the coming Thursday service. Looney Louie had a terrible accident that broke both of his arms soon afterward. Big Tony made sure Looney Louie made all of Pastor Tom's services in the coming weeks and never again was the preacher's life threatened at the prison.

Two months later, Big Tony from New Jersey was released. He received a special private thank you from the Warden in his office, along with the keys to a car waiting in the employee parking lot. Both men knew The Voice rewarded those completed successfully the work he gave them. Above all else, they knew you never wanted to disappoint the Voice.

The following day, Big Tony waited in his new car parked in the visitor's lot at the prison. He was expecting someone—someone he knew and wanted was being released today. About two o'clock, Leo, one of his snitches who had been the prison librarian, left the jailhouse. He was with another man Big Tony had seen in the prison but knew little about. Leo walked to Big Tony's car that had blackout windows. Big Tony rolled one down about three inches and watched the men approach. He called out, "Leo." Leo looked around nervously, but could not see where the voice calling his name came from. Big Tony called out again, "Leo, over here." Leo saw Big Tony, motioned for the other man to stay back and walked to the car. "Leo, you still looking for something to do like we talked about?"

"Yeah, I am. You got those sneakers I wanted?"

"Sure do."

Leo looked at the top of the line Nike sneakers with Michael Jordan's name on the side, and he smiled. "Looks like we got a deal. Hey, that's my friend, Chad. He was my assistant at the library. I think he read every book on history, local to national, we had. Needs a lift to Cumberland. I can vouch for him. Is that okay?"

Big Tony looked hard at him. "I don't like surprises. You know that." He paused. "But if he's a friend of yours, that tells me a lot. So yeah, he can have a lift."

"Thanks, you won't regret this," said Leo.

Big Tony hoped he wouldn't. "Get in. I have that burner phone you need for business, and it's got lots of minutes." *Don't* lose it. And no shop talk when that guy's with us, understand?"

"Gotcha." Leo whistled to Chad and waved his hand for him to come. They got in the four-door sedan, and Big Tony drove to the main entrance and noticed a sizeable historical marker which read, 'On this site sat Fort Nichols, one link in a chain of frontier forts George Washington ordered built for defense during the French and

Indian War.' *Those forts were all over this area*, thought Big Tony. They pulled out onto Maryland Route 220 and left Western Maryland Correctional Institute in their rearview mirror. Ten minutes later, they dropped Chad off at a rundown house on Independence Street and drove to another house in the Mapleside neighborhood and parked on the street.

"This is the place I was telling you about. You know what I need you to do. Just do what I want, and don't screw it up, *capiche*?"

"Yeah, I understand. You can count on me."

"No surprises, remember?"

"Yeah, no surprises."

Leo got out of the car and waved goodbye as he walked up the steps to the house. He knocked, and an old woman opened the door a little. She saw Big Tony, smiled and let Leo in. As she closed the door, Big Tony saw her wink. Lois would take care of him. She knew what to do, and this one needed watching. Keep your friends close and your enemies even closer. This one had asked too many questions about Tom Kenney and Braddock's gold. The librarian at the prison had seen enough information to put him on the radar screen. His boss, the Voice, wanted the treasure for himself, and nothing better come between it and him. It was not healthy to disappoint the Voice. Big Tony knew that, but others did not. Some people learned the hard way.

Sometime later

It had been a good morning until he received the phone call. The number indicated it was Big Tony, but why would he be calling at this time? "Boss," he said. "I have some news. Leo,, the snitch, is dead."

The Voice thought it might come to this, but what came next was a surprise. Big Tony said, "The Cumberland Police found him floating face down in the Potomac River near Candoc, and he had a knife in his back. None of us had anything to do with it."

The Voice pondered this development. *Someone had killed Leo before they had found it necessary, but who and why?* Big Tony went on, "Now the bad news, there was no mention of finding his cell phone, and he was shoeless."

The Voice did not like the sound of this, and it grew even worse. Big Tony said, "The GPS I planted in his shoes is still active, and it's moving. No boss, it's not floating down the river. It's moving through the streets of LaVale on old Route 40 now. I'll intercept it in the Narrows near Kline's Restaurant. We should find out what's up then."

***

Big Tony watched as the car went by Kline's Restaurant, located in the Narrows. Chad, 'Leo's friend,' was driving, and the GPS moved with the vehicle. Chad had to be wearing Leo's special shoes. Big Tony pulled out behind the car, but a minivan slipped between them, and it was just as well. Big Tony needed some cover for his developing plan. The vehicles stopped at a red light, and Big Tony called the cell phone he had given Leo. He watched as Chad jumped in the car. The phone had an extreme vibrate mode, and it had Chad's attention and Big Tony's too. He now knew what happened to Leo, and he didn't like where this could be leading. He called the boss and informed him of the situation. The Voice told him to keep him updated. Big Tony would know what to do.

Chapter 23

Yes, it was an interesting day. He'd been running one of the local routes, and it gave him time to touch base with a lot of his customers. All but one seemed pleased with the Knobley Mountain Bottled Water and service. That one had always been difficult and wanted to haggle over price. They finally agreed, if he ordered larger quantities less often, Tom could give him a better deal. Both went away happy with the new arrangement.

On the way out of Cumberland, coming home in the afternoon, Tom stopped at several establishments on WV Route 28. Linda's Old Furnace Restaurant and the market next door would be the last two. The latter needed their usual amount. He stood by his truck parked along the side of the building and noted two men looking at something just over the guard rail near the WV Historical Marker for Fort Sellers. He loaded his industrial grade hand truck, and the gray-haired men walked toward him. Tom asked, "What did you guys find over there? Dead possum?"

They smiled and said, "No dead animals. We're geocaching."

"Geo-what?" asked Tom.

"A geocache. It's kind of like a treasure hunt. Someone places a cache for other people to find. You use GPS. There're several different websites on the internet that tell you where and how. It's fun and gets us out of the house. Our wives were driving us crazy, and it sure beats playin' cards and drinkin'."

"Sounds interesting. I'll have to try it when I get time, whenever that is."

"Yeah, I remember what having a job was like, but I tell you this, retirement is what you make it. I've been so busy I don't know when

I ever had time for work. Some people think you sit around all day with nuthin' to do, but if you want to catch me, you better make an appointment."

"Gotcha. Thanks for the info on geocaching. I think I'd like to try it someday when I get the chance."

"You'll enjoy it. See ya. Have a blessed day."

"You, too."

The men got into a car and left. Tom loaded up the order for the restaurant and took it inside. He put it in the backroom and stopped at the counter near the cash register. Tom gave the cashier the bill and then sat down to a coffee and apple pie waiting for him. He took a bite of it and finished the cup of coffee off in one gulp.

The waitress named Debbie shook her head. "Well, I see you still have that OCD thingy," she said.

"Yup. You know me too well. OCD, Obsessive Coffee Disease, and you know the only cure for that, right?

She made a face and nodded her head. "Yes, Tom. The only cure is what else? More coffee." She poured him another cup.

"Right as rain, Doctor Debbie. You got it."

She went on to some other customers at the bar counter. Tom recognized one man, Mr. Whitacre, and Tom spoke to him. "Mr. Whitacre, I haven't seen you in a while. What brings you here?"

"Food. What do you think? Wife's on a health kick again, and it's like to killing me. Doc says I'm too heavy, my sugars and blood pressures up, so she cut my portions to nothing. I'll be so healthy, but she's starving me to death in the process."

They made small talk for a while as Tom finished his snack. He left a five-dollar bill sticking out from under the coffee cup, said goodbye to Mr. Whitacre, who joyfully chowed down on a hot beef sandwich covered with mashed potatoes and brown gravy and departed. At the truck, he placed the hand cart in its spot and secured it. He walked around the truck, climbed up to the cab and opened the door.

"Get in," growled a man's voice. "And keep your mouth shut if you know what's good for you.

Tom stared into the barrel of a Smith and Wesson 9 mm pistol. He did as he was told.

"Now," the man said, "ease the truck outta here and head down Old Furnace Road."

Tom pulled the truck around and drove across the parking lot. He stopped, looked both ways, and turned left onto the road. A short distance later, he passed the old iron furnace that gave the area and road its name. "What do you want and who are you?" Tom asked.

The man sniffed through his nose. "The name's not important, and I think you know what I want."

Tom glanced at the man and the gun. He was about thirty and looked somewhat familiar, but Tom kept this to himself. He scratched the scabs on his arms. *Must be a meth head,* thought Tom. *This isn't going to end well.* Tom noted the expensive sneakers he was wearing. "Nice shoes," he said.

The young man sneered, "Got 'em from a friend," and then he laughed sarcastically.

They traveled another mile or so down the winding road, passing a small family cemetery and a no-name bar, and then the young man jumped. With his left hand, he reached into his shirt pocket and pulled out a cell phone. He said, "Damn things been going off all day." He pushed the off switch. "Won't have to worry with that anymore today." He slipped it back in his pocket.

Tom continued to drive over the twisting country road and thought about what he could do. He could throw the truck into a spin and flip it, but neither he nor his passenger were wearing a seat belt. They would probably both be tossed out and run over by the truck if Tom did not get shot when he swerved the truck. *Not a good idea. Gotta be something else,* so he drove on.

"Turn left here," the young man said.

Just as I expected. We're heading for the old farm, and he thinks I know where the gold is. This ain't gonna be pretty, thought Tom.

They went through the sleepy little town of Patterson Creek. "Turn right after the white house," the young man said.

Tom looked at him. "We're going to the farm, aren't we?"

The young man smiled sarcastically. "You're a smart guy, and you know what I want, don't you?"

Tom nodded. There had to be a plan to save him, but what was it? A feeling of gloom came over Tom, and he had a bad feeling in the pit of his stomach. *God help me;* he silently prayed.

Tom turned on the side road that led down past an odorous barn to the creek. They went over the low water bridge. How Tom wished he could be fishing today instead of in the truck with this crazy man. They rode to the sharp left-hand turn and began the sharp ascent to the top of the north end of Patterson Creek Ridge. One mile later, they came to the country lane that led to the old farmhouse where Tom had been shot, and two other men had died. Tom pulled in and stopped at the gate. The young man looked at Tom and waved the gun around. "I know you have a key. Get out and open the gate."

"I…" Tom started to say he did not have a key but felt it best not to argue with the spacey man. He got out and went to the gate. Much to his surprise, he found it had been very cleverly dummy locked. He couldn't believe his luck. Tom turned his back to the truck and concealed his work. He swung the gate open, walked back to the truck, and climbed in.

"See how easy that was. Do the same for the rest of what I want, and it'll be a good day."

Maybe for you, but not for me. Tom still could not see how he would get out of this with his skin intact. *God help me.*

As they drove up the lane, Tom began to remember coming here the day he was shot. He saw the faces of the two men who were shot, and then he thought he heard the sound of a Huey helicopter. They neared the old farmhouse with crime scene tape still around it. "Stop the truck and get out," ordered the man who had scratched his arms bloody. "Now, go over there."

Tom did as he was told.

"Now, I haven't got all day. Where's the gold? I know it's here and you know where. Where is it?"

The air seemed thick and hot. The sky seemed to spin, and Tom nearly fell. He looked at the man and said, "I don't know."

The man cursed and pointed the gun at Tom. "Tell me where it is, or I'll shot you now and shot you again and again till you tell me. I know how to make a man feel pain and wish he was dead."

The faces of men he saw die in the Ia Drang Valley in Vietnam flashed in front of him. He looked at the man waving the gun. "I don't know."

The young man snarled, pointed the gun at Tom, and fired. The bullet whizzed by Tom's head, and he dropped to the ground. The man angrily charged him and held the gun to his head. "Changed my mind. I'm not gonna tell you again. I'm gonna count to three, and if I don't hear what I wanna hear, I gonna put a round in your head."

"One."

"I can't remember."

"Two."

"I don't know!"

"THREE!"

A shot rang out, and the young man fell on the ground next to Tom. He looked at the man. There was a blood spot on his head where a bullet had entered. His face turned into Chris Benally's, and it spoke, "Tell my dad, I died in battle." The eyes closed, and Tom closed his own eyes. "No," he said over and over. "No," and he began to cry.

A little time passed. Tom was able to compose himself, and he looked around. The dead man was still dead, and two men were approaching him. They carried M16s with sniper scopes and silencers. Both were dressed in camouflage fatigues and had white sacks on their heads with eye holes cut out like the two men who tried to kill him before. They walked up to Tom. He asked, "Do you intend to kill me now?"

The men looked at each other, and one spoke, but the voice sounded like one coming from a mechanical speaking aid someone with throat cancer would use. "Mr. Kenney, sorry you do not understand. This man was going to kill you, and we saved your life. As I told you, I am your Benefactor. No harm will come to you or your family while you are under my protection. I want the treasure that is in your head, nothing more."

Jay Heavner

"Whatever you say. Whatever you say." Tom stood up, but his legs would not hold him. He twisted and passed out on the ground.

The second man looked down at Tom. He gently nudged him with his foot. Tom was out like a light. The man shook his covered head. "Looks like his PTSD has kicked in again. Shame, he's a man I respect."

"Yes. Load him in the truck and take him down where the road parallels the railroad tracks. Leave the truck and him there. We will call 911 when we are safely away and as usual, leave nothing for the cops to go on how he got there. We will clean up the mess here, and then I will follow you to the drop off point."

"Sounds like a plan. I told you Chap and Leo needed watching. You need to see those books on Braddock's gold need to be removed from the prison library. I hope they haven't created more problems, but who knows.

"Yes, I'll see the message goes to the warden tomorrow morning. We can hope these two were the only curious ones. If there are more, they can be dealt with too, if necessary."

Big Tony nodded his bag-covered head." Boss, do you think he'll ever remember?"

"He will. Everything comes to he who waits. I can feel it. He knows where the treasure is, and he will tell me."

"You've never been wrong before, boss. You've never been wrong before."

***

The next day

Oh, my head hurts. Tom looked around. *Where am I? No wonder it looked familiar.* He was in the VA Hospital in Cumberland, again. *How did I get here?* He didn't know. He turned his head to the side and saw Joann seated on the other side of the room away from him. At times like these, he could be aggressive when he awoke. "Jo?" he said. "How long have I been out?"

She approached him carefully to study his demeanor. "They brought you in yesterday. Someone saw your truck down on Dan's

Run Road and gave 911 a call. The cops found you slumped on your seat."

"I don't know how I got there."

"How do you feel?"

"I got a splitting headache, but other than that, I think I'm okay. What did the doctors say?"

"PTSD again. They said once you awoke, they would observe you for a while, and if all went well, you could be released."

"Thank God."

"The cops have a question for you."

"What is it?"

"They found a drop of fresh blood on the seat, and it wasn't yours. They're going to send it off and see if it matches anything in their database. Any idea who's it is or how it got there?"

"No, I don't, but I have this feeling it has something to do with Braddock's gold again."

She nodded her head and said, "I think so too, and so do the cops."

Tom was silent.

She asked, "What are you thinking?"

He looked at her. "Paul was right."

"Are you okay, honey?"

"Yes, the apostle Paul told Timothy 'the love of money is the root of all kinds of evil.' Did he ever get it right on that one."

Joann nodded and pulled herself close to him. "Somehow honey, we'll get through this. If God is for us, who can be against us?"

Tom said, "It'll work out. Somehow, it'll all work out."

//
Chapter 24

Two months later

What a week it had been. This week started out like so many Tom had recently. It was like having three Mondays in a row. Everything seemed to happen in threes. On Monday, one of the trucks blew a tire at 55 mph, and the driver, Jared, had barely been able to keep the vehicle under control in the emergency stop. It took all day to get the tire truck out for service, so his route started out the week a day behind. On Tuesday, Andy's truck died in downtown Cumberland traffic and what a mess that had been. Fortunately, he wasn't given a ticket, but the truck had to be towed in and worked on. A faulty crankshaft positioning sensor proved the problem. All in all, Tom figured this cost the company at least a thousand bucks in lost time, towing fees, mechanic shop fees, equipment downtime, and wages. Today, in the late afternoon, when the man who called himself his Benefactor phoned, Tom almost welcomed the change.

As usual, Tom's phone had shown 000-000-0000 as the calling number. He left the warehouse to take the call at the employee's picnic table outside.

"Hello to my Benefactor. I hope your week has gone better than mine."

The Benefactor seemed surprised. "How so?" The computer-generated voice asked.

"It's been a rotten week so far," said Tom. "I've had two trucks break down, both expensive, and I think I may be getting a cold. Either that or my sinuses are acting up again."

"I am sorry to hear that, but you need to beware. It is commonly said misfortunes come in threes."

Tom said, "I'm quite aware of that. Just hoping the third shoe to fall won't be as expensive or drastic." He stopped. "I know you didn't call me to talk about the weather or broken-down trucks. Just what is it that's on your mind today?"

"The usual, of course. Have you remembered where the treasure is?"

"No, I don't know where Braddock's Gold is buried, but you know about me being found passed out in my truck?"

"Yes, I knew about that."

"And there was someone's blood on the seat that wasn't mine."

The Benefactor was surprised. They had missed that. Even the best plan can have holes in it. He said flatly, "That is interesting."

"Also, I'm having flashbacks of driving up to the farmhouse at Patterson Creek. It's crazy, but one is me alone in my pickup and the other's with a young man pointing a gun at me, and we're in one of my business trucks. Then it goes blank."

There was a brief pause between the two men. "Is that all?" asked the Benefactor.

"That's all. I wish there was more. It gets very frustrating with these holes in my memory."

"Let me fill you in a little. You have been to the farm, not once, but twice. The first time was when you were shot and received that scar on your head a year or so ago. The second was just before you were found unconscious in your truck several months past. You see, Mr. Kenney, I've been watching out for you. Someone else was willing to kill you for the information you have in your head. He is now very dead."

Tom was shocked. "Do you mean to tell me the young man I saw in the flashbacks wanted to kill me? It was real and not a hallucination?"

"That is correct, Mr. Kenney. He will not harm anyone anymore, ever. I believe you will find it is his blood on the truck seat."

There was silence from Tom for a long moment, and then The Benefactor asked, "Mr. Kenney? Mr. Kenney, are you there?"

"Yes, I'm here." He paused again. "I need to know something."

"Certainly, Mr. Kenney. What is it?"

"I gotta know. Did I kill him?"

The Benefactor was surprised again. "No, Mr. Kenney, you did not kill him. I was there with my associate when the target was eliminated." He heard a sigh of relief on the phone. There was another period of silence. "Mr. Kenney, are you still there?"

"Yes, I'm still here, and I was just wondering why. Guess I'll die at the appointed time when Morty comes calling."

"Would you explain yourself, Mr. Kenney? And who is this Morty?"

"My Bible tells me there is a season for everything—a time for joy, and a time for sorrow, a time to be born, and a time to die. Morty is our friend mortality. He comes calling for about 7,000 Americans each and every day. Rain or shine, cold or hot, it don't matter to Morty. I've felt him near numerous times in my life—several times growing up when I believed I was invincible. He was there, everywhere in the three days of battle in the Ia Drang Valley in Vietnam. He was there at the farm when I got this scar on my head from a bullet meant to kill me, and he was there, waiting, waiting for me again just two months ago. I don't know why I'm not dead other than that same Bible in Hebrews 9:27 tells me, 'There is appointed a time for all to die and then face judgment,' and I guess it was just not my time."

A long silence followed. Now it was Tom's turn to ask, "My Benefactor, are you there?"

"Yes, I'm here." The words choked in his throat, and he barely got them out. How well he knew about old Morty. He'd seen men die. There was no denying the finality of this life. Something was stirring inside the man—something he hadn't felt in years. "Please," he said. "Please continue telling me what you believe."

The preacher in Tom could not help but speak. "What do I believe? Are God's promises true, or are they comforting myths? If they are just myths, there can be no real comfort in them. Christ Jesus, who shed his precious blood on a cruel Roman cross said, 'I give them eternal life, and they shall *never* perish. No one can snatch them out of my hand.' He goes on, 'In this world, you will have troubles. But take heart! I have overcome the world.' There's a ton of other scriptures like these. God is good and faithful in all ways. If Morty and me held hands and I slipped into eternity today, I'd come to rest in God's hand. His peace can be nothing short of amazing. It's sustained me through all of my troubles. When I am weak, He's always strong."

Tom continued, "Our days on this Earth are numbered and short. What is important? God? Our family? Relationship with others? Everything will amount to little in the end, but still, we must live our lives and strive to do our best. Honor God in all we do and do it with all our heart and excellence. What will matter ten thousand years from now, and what won't? Old Morty can help us get clarity on that. Our lives are but a vapor, here in the morning, and soon gone. Morty can be a servant who points us to the One who holds all life in His hands. So what do you say, Benefactor? If Morty comes calling on you today, are you ready?"

After a short lull, The Benefactor spoke. "Mr. Kenney, you are an interesting person. You have given me much to think about. I look forward to our next conversation. I will consider what you have said. And Mr. Kenney, some of your memory seems to be coming back. See if you can remember where Braddock's Gold is. You are no good to me dead."

The phone clicked, and a dial tone sounded. Tom now knew why they hadn't killed him. He was no good to him dead. But if he remembered where the gold was and told them, would they let him live then? They'd have no further use for him, and he could be a liability. *Would The Benefactor be true to his word? Could he be trusted or not?* Tom had little more than a feeling the answer was yes, but he'd been wrong before when he put his faith in people. Only God was totally faithful to His word. Tom shut his phone off. He didn't want to talk with to anyone. Tom wanted to think. *What did he need to do before Morty came calling on him?*

Tom sat at the picnic bench for a long time. There was much to consider. A shadow came over him. He realized the sun had gone behind Knobley Mountain. A look at his watch told him it was almost supper time. He walked to the main door of the warehouse. It was locked, and everyone had gone home. *Wonder what Joann has for supper?*

Tom walked over to the farmhouse he called home and opened the door. The smell of spaghetti sauce filled his nose. It was his favorite. Joann had somehow wrangled the recipe out of the cook, Mrs. Cheshire, at the grade school. Tom had loved it since he was a kid. He walked into the dining room and saw the best china set out, candles, a delicious looking tossed salad waiting, and two glasses filled with white wine. They were going to be eating high on the hog tonight. Joann came into the room from the hall. *Must have been in the bathroom,* he thought.

"There you are, my Prince. I hope everything meets your satisfaction."

"Looks great to this ole meat and taters kind of guy."

"Sit down, and I'll serve you. I know it's been a rough week. You could use a change in your life," she said. "And Miriah's spending the night with her cousins."

"Those girls get along good, and yes, I could use some change. This week's been crazy with the trucks breaking down, and then today The Benefactor called. We talked for a long time. Somehow, I think the man's tired of his life, and he's searching for meaning in it and coming up empty. Strange, how I can have empathy for a man I should fear."

The meal was excellent. They made small talk as they ate. Afterward, they put the leftovers in the refrigerator and placed the dirty dishes in the dishwasher. The new one they installed a month ago cleaned like a hurricane. Tom went into the living room and sat down. Joann came in and snuggled up next to him. "You wanna have some fun tonight? We're all alone."

"Sounds like a great idea to me, but I can tell when something's up. You're holding something back from me. Spit it out. What's up?"

She looked into his eyes and said, "Tom, I'm pregnant."

The End

Psalms 91:3 For it is He who delivers you from the snare of the hunter. And from the deadly pestilence.

WANT TO READ MORE?

Braddock's Gold Mystery Series

Braddock's Gold

Hunter's Moon

Fool's Wisdom

Killing Darkness

Florida Murder Mystery Series

Death at Windover

Murder at the Canaveral Diner

Murder at the Indian River

WANT TO HELP THE AUTHOR?

If you enjoyed the book, would you help get the word out? Please tell others about it. Word-of-mouth advertising is the best marketing tool on this planet.

A good review on Amazon, Goodreads, or elsewhere would help with the author being able to keep writing full time. It doesn't have to be long. Thanks.

SIGN UP FOR JAY HEAVNER'S NEWSLETTER

With this, Jay will occasionally keep you informed with new books coming out and anything else special. Feel free to email him at jay@jayheavner.com. His website is www.jayheavner.com. He loves reader feedback.

Fool's Wisdom, Book three in Braddock's Gold novel series

Chapter 1

April 1965

At the Kenney home place along WV Route 28, Short Gap, WV

Tom Kenney sat at the table in the old farmhouse he'd known as home his whole life. He was having a hard time sorting out all the information his father had just given him. When his father told him he needed to talk with him, his heart sank lower than whale dung in the deepest ocean. His worst fears were realized. His father had found out about the events of last Saturday, and he was a dead man. His father was going to read him the riot act. He was dead meat and would be grounded for life or longer. And worse of all, he'd disappointed the man who cared for and raised him after his mother had died when he was small. He could not bear the look he knew was coming. Still, there was something exciting about what he'd been a part of. It felt what a drug addiction must be like. That both frightened him and thrilled him.

His father sat down at the table and had a manila folder in his hand. He laid it in front of Tom and told him to open it. Tom was sure it was evidence of his misdeeds. Instead, the first thing he saw was a picture of his mother at about age sixteen. My, she was a beauty. He could see why his Dad liked her at first sight. She had long dark hair, light olive skin, and dark, almost coal-black eyes that shined like two embers in her head. And at the bottom in the margin, someone had written in ink, "Goodland Cherokee Orphanage School." Tom looked up from the picture with surprise. His Dad said, "Tom, it's time I told you about your mother. I know you don't remember much about her. You were so young when she passed. It was hard on you and harder on me. There will never be a better woman created on this earth. The cancer took her from us way too soon."

He stopped and wiped a tear from his cheek. "I still miss her dancing eyes and sweet smile. How she ever kept those in that hole they called a school, I'll never know. But she did, and that's what first attracted her to me. I had just returned from military service with Uncle Sam in Europe after WWII. One of the soldiers I fought alongside of through France and Germany told me of his home in North Carolina and asked me if I wanted to have some R and R, you know, Rest and Relaxation time in the mountains there. It sounded like a pretty good idea to me, a cot and meals and no one shooting at me. So we went from the port in Norfolk, Virginia, by bus to the hills, I mean the mountains of western North Carolina. I thought we had mountains here in WV, and we do have them all over the state, but those mountains seemed like they went up to the very face of God. My buddy got us jobs working at the Indian Orphanage. He was a good talker. He could sell refrigerators to the Eskimos. He told them we were all-round handymen, and soon we were fixin' up that old place best we could and learning how to do it as we went. It didn't take me long to see this place was no paradise. The government's policy with Indians at that time was to de-Indian the Indian out of the Indian to save the Indian. I saw some of the kids beaten if they spoke Cherokee or did anything that had any Indian attached to it.

It was there I met your Mom. She told me she was dropped off at the orphanage when she was just a baby. She never knew who her parents were, but from what little records she found, she was either full blood Cherokee or at least half. To make a long story short, we fell in love. She was sixteen at the time. With the money I saved up, I bought an old rattle-trap car, and we used it to make our escape from the orphanage.

No one ever looked for her. They were happy to be rid of another mouth to feed. She'd have to leave anyway as soon as she came of age. With her looks, she could pass for a white person, and that's what we did when we got home here. Your grandpa, I think, suspected something was up, but he never did say anything. We lived in this old house with my maw and paw for many years. When they got old and feeble, she was the one who took care of them. She was a good woman. You came along in 1947, and she now had three besides herself to care for. I don't know how she did it, but she did. She was a fine woman, like one of those virtuous women they talk about in the Bible."

"So what I wanted to tell you was, Tom, you are either half Cherokee or at least a quarter. Back then, there was kind of a bad stigma in being mixed race, and I know there still is some, but this is something I thought you were ready for."

Tom looked stunned and said so. He looked at the other pictures in the folder. Each one had his mother in it. Some were with his dad. Some had her with his grandparents. A few were group pictures, and a few were of him with his mother. Tom wanted to tear up when he saw these, but he fought it. The youth didn't want anyone to think he was not manly. Sissies cried. His father saw this turmoil in Tom but said nothing. He knew what was going on in the young man.

Finally, his dad said, "I'll leave you here with these for now so you can look at them. I got to get off to work."

He rose from the table and headed for the door. He grabbed his coat and hat off the clothes pole by the back door. Tom notices a little tremor in his Dad's right hand. Then he turned to Tom and dryly said, "Try to stay out of trouble today." And with that, he was gone.

Tom's stomach churned a little. The story must have really shaken his dad up as his hands had always been so steady and firm. And it seemed his dad knew more than he was saying, or did he? He looked at the pictures for another ten minutes or so and then heard the wheels of the black 57 Chevy on the dirt and gravel coming up to the house. It stopped around the back, and the driver honked the horn. Tom took one last look at the first picture he had seen in the folder, the picture of his mother. He sighed and closed the folder. Tom grabbed his coat and ball hat of the clothes pole and headed out the back door.

"Hey, buddy, you look like you saw a ghost. You okay?" questioned the driver.

"Yeah, I'll be alright. I just heard some surprising news. It'll all work out, somehow. You still want to go through with this?"

"Damn straight. I wouldn't miss this for the world," the driver replied.

"Then, let's do it. I love it when a plan comes together."

The driver smiled a satisfied grin. "Then, what's keeping us? Let's get with it."

The driver backed up the hot rod, put it in Drive, went down the gravel and dirt driveway, stopped at WV Route 28, waited for a truck heading for Fort Ashby to go by, then turned left and headed toward Cumberland, Maryland and their day with destiny.

Made in the USA
Middletown, DE
09 September 2025